MY UNEXPECTED SURPRISE

PIPER RAYNE

Cover Design: By Hang Le

Cover Photo: Wander Aguiar Photography

1st Line Editor: Joy Editing

2nd Line Editor: My Brother's Editor

Proofreader: My Brother's Editor

About My Unexpected Surprise

I never thought of myself as dad material.

Until my one-night stand showed up in my small Alaskan town five months pregnant.

But I don't shy away from responsibility. First, because I'm a Greene and not to boast but we're kind of a big deal in Sunrise Bay. Second, I'm the Sheriff.

I couldn't have predicted how protective I'd become for the safety of her and my unborn baby to the point of asking her to move in with me and be my roommate.

Just when I think I have the situation under control, another surprise knocks me over, but it only spurs me to double down.

I'll be the first to admit, I didn't think it through. Somewhere between the dinners, the TV show binging, the doctor appointments, and me walking in on her naked, lines blurred.

In what feels like warp speed, my bachelor for life status is in jeopardy and I'm fighting for the most important thing of all—my family.

my unexpected SURPRISE

The Greenes

Hank's Kids

Cade Greene (33)
Co-owner Truth or Dare Brewery
Fisher Greene (31)
Sheriff
Xavier Greene (29)
Pro Football Player
Adam Greene (27)
Forest Ranger
Chevelle Greene (26)
Water Boat Tourist

Marla's Kids

Jed Greene (33)
Co-owner of Truth or Dare Brewery
Nikki Greene (30)
Radio Host
Mandi Greene (28)
Owner of SunBay Inn
Posey Greene (24)
Owner of Fringe

Hank and Marla's Kid

Rylan Greene (13)

Chapter One

Fisher

The bagpipes play "Amazing Grace" and I straighten up, bowing my head.

Nothing prepares you for watching a fellow police officer get buried after being shot in the line of duty. Our small unit is honoring a fallen officer from the neighboring town of Greywall, where a traffic stop with a drunk fisherman went wrong. I didn't know him personally, but I've heard enough stories to know he was a good cop.

I didn't come to the realization that I wanted to be a cop until I was due to graduate high school and felt pressured to figure out my life goals. But being a police officer suits me. I can be gruff and abrasive sometimes and I don't have a lot of sympathy for people who break the law. Though my high school buddies still have a problem believing it sometimes. God knows I never obeyed the law when I was a pimple-faced kid.

I think it was the fact that my mom died under the ice of a frozen lake because no one could reach her fast enough that spurred me to seek a career as a first responder. Maybe I thought I could prevent some other kid from losing their mom. Instead, I have to face the reality that because of our job, my coworkers may never come home to their kids.

We stand like soldiers and stare down at the casket. I

guarantee each one of us is thinking about how it could have easily been any of us in that silk-lined box. The fallen officer's wife clings to her small children while she sobs uncontrollably. Both kids' faces look like stone, and it's hard to tell whether they comprehend the atomic bomb that just imploded the life they once knew.

I was once them.

Nausea bubbles up in my stomach like a witch's cauldron, and I choke back the urge to vomit.

Members from the Greywall Police fold up the flag that is lying across the casket and hand her the triangle of fabric. The wife releases a deep wail that's eerily similar to Chevelle's the night of my mom's death.

Patrick groans beside me. He's got a wife and three kids at home. He coaches football for his boys and basketball for his girl. If you look up dad in the dictionary, there should be a picture of him.

After the preacher says amen, most of us say our goodbyes and descend the hill of the cemetery.

"Tara's freaking out," Patrick whispers. "She's shook."

I'm not surprised his wife is out of sorts. Things like this hit a little too close to home. "She'll calm down. It's a shock because it's affirmation that it can happen to any of us any day."

"Thanks for the encouraging words, Sheriff."

I take one last glimpse over my shoulder at the young mother and her children. Who I assume are family members are rounding up the kids and helping her to turn away from the grave. Today won't even be the hardest day. It's worse weeks from now, when the meal shares stop and everyone else goes on with their lives. That's when the gaping void the deceased left behind really becomes apparent.

"Like I said, she'll calm down. Give her a few days."

Patrick raises a skeptical eyebrow at me and pats my shoulder. "Have a good night. I gotta head in for my shift."

"See you tomorrow morning." I head to my truck.

Patrick's just another example of why marriage and police officers don't work. His wife is worried, and she should be, but what kind of life is that for her? Presley's not freaking out every time Cade goes to the brewery. Maybe if I retire early I'll think about finding someone to tie myself to for life, but then again, I'll be so over the hill I'll be skiing down the other side toward the finish line because I love my job and don't see it ending anytime soon.

I pull my phone from my pocket and see ten messages from various family members. Can't they just send one message in the group chat? I go to my dad's text first, knowing his message will be straightforward and get right to the point.

> Dad: We're pretty sure Emilia broke her arm.
> All headed to the hospital.

I frown and scroll down, finding another message.

> Dad: We're leaving, she's all casted up.
> They'll be there for a little longer if you get
> this soon. Otherwise go to Jed's house if
> you want to see her.

When I check the time, I realize that last message came in a minute ago, so I head toward the hospital.

After I stop at the store to buy Emilia balloons since the hospital gift shop will be closed, a text comes through. I'm stopped at a light before the hospital entrance, so I take a quick look.

Jed: You been to the hospital lately?

> Heard what happened. Stopped to get E
> something. Almost there.

Per Jed's usual MO he isn't being shy about asking why I'm not there yet. But Emilia is my niece and I stopped for balloons because we share a kinship—we're both motherless. Plus, she lived with us until Jed and Molly recently bought a house in downtown Sunrise Bay, leaving me alone in my parents' old house. It's still weird to come home to a quiet place after living with some of my brothers for years. One by one, they've all found their match and moved on with their lives.

I pull into the hospital parking lot and park, then climb out with balloons in hand and mentally prepare myself for the razzing I'll take for purchasing congratulation balloons and not get-well ones. I find Jed standing outside the entrance.

"Can you believe all they had at the store were congratulations balloons? But I figure she'd love the balloons anyway, right?"

He looks as if he's minutes away from throwing up.

Anxiety fires like a slingshot through my blood. "How is she? Why are you so pale? Did something happen? Is it serious?"

My dad said it was just a broken arm. Did he get it wrong? Then again, Jed is pretty fiercely protective of his little girl.

"She's fine. It's a broken arm." Jed doesn't make any motion to move, so I walk past him into the hospital. It's practically my third home after the station and my house.

I say hello to Fran at the nurses' station, but she's quick

to dismiss me. Must be the full moon tonight. Shit always gets weird around here during the full moon.

I excuse myself and walk back over to Jed. "What room is Emilia in?"

The loud squealing sound of shoes on the linoleum pulls my attention from Jed toward the end of the hall.

Allie.

I freeze. I haven't seen her in months, not even here at the hospital. Last I was told, she took a leave. My gaze falls down her body, but I only make it to her swollen belly before I feel as if a wallet is lodged in my throat. My stomach turns over, then it feels as if the floor drops out from beneath me. "What the fuck?"

"Fisher," Allie says with the same meek voice as mine.

Molly peeks out of a door midway down the hall. Jed rocks back on his heels with a small groan. Is this why he's so pasty white?

"What the hell is going on?" I ask.

Allie's hand falls to her stomach. The bouquet of balloons floats a few inches toward the ceiling before Jed catches the multicolored ribbons. I approach Allie, gently grasp her elbow, and lead her right into Emilia's room.

Emilia's eyes light up when she sees me, but I turn Allie around and point at her belly. "What is that?"

"A baby," she answers, as if I asked her what color the sky is.

I mentally count how many months it's been since the last time we were together. "*Whose* baby?"

You'd never guess we're in a hospital from how library quiet the room is. Jed and Molly watch on as though we're the season finale of their favorite TV drama.

"Yours."

My heart plummets as if there's an anchor attached and

it's falling to the darkest depths of the ocean. A million different reactions bombard me all at once, but I can't distinguish one feeling over another. Anger that she hid the pregnancy from me. Pissed off that I got her pregnant. Sadness—

"Baby!" Emilia exclaims.

Jed hands the bouquet of balloons back to me. "Looks like these are for you after all."

The balloons slowly float to the florescent-lighted ceiling because I can't even feel my fingers right now to grip them.

Molly slowly steps forward and tugs Jed back to her side as though he's her child.

I eye Allie with disdain. "Care to explain?"

"I could ask you the same question." She puts her hands over her belly as though she's protecting it from harm, and that pisses me off further. I'm the baby's goddamn father. It's insulting.

"We need to talk." The words barely make it past my lips, my jaw is clenched so hard.

"Baby!" Emilia shouts again.

"Shh..." Molly whispers, but Emilia is in a baby-loving phase. All she asked for for her birthday was a baby stroller and a high chair.

"I need to start my shift." Allie steps back.

Fear grips me by the throat and squeezes. If I let her out of my sight, will she flee?

"You aren't going anywhere," I say with more authority than I should.

"I didn't break the law, Fisher, you can't arrest me." She crosses her arms and juts out a hip.

Goddammit, I forgot how infuriating Allie can be. Just as stubborn as me. "Why didn't you tell me you were pregnant?"

She glances to the left where Jed and Molly stand, then

her gaze falls to the floor. "Can we please do this somewhere else?"

"Fine." I step forward to usher her out into the hall.

"I can't right now, Fisher, I have to work. But I'll meet you tomorrow or something."

"After your shift," I say.

She nods, dodging eye contact. "I get off at three."

"You shouldn't be working these late shifts."

Her eyes brim with anger. "Don't go acting like you care about me now. I'll see you at three." She turns her back on me and stalks off down the hallway.

I step forward to go after her, but a hand on my chest stops me. I look over to find Jed there.

"Give her some space," he says.

"Space? She's had space for five fucking months."

Emilia points at me. "Bad word!"

"It won't be the last one I say in front of you," I grumble.

"She's not going anywhere. She's working," Jed says.

I blow out a breath and sit in a chair. Who would've predicted that Jed would be the calm one in a messed-up situation like this?

The clock reads four in the afternoon. Damn it. I have to wait eleven hours before I get my answers. This will try my patience.

"So, Daddy, are you hoping for a girl or a boy?" Jed asks.

Molly pinches him and he yelps.

"Gotta say, I never thought of you as a dad." He sits in the chair next to me.

I rest my forearms on my knees and run my hands through my hair. "Neither did I."

It's actually my worst fucking nightmare.

Chapter Two

Allie

I'm jumpy my whole shift. My coworkers probably think it's because I'm no longer used to working in a hospital setting, but they'd be wrong. I have to face Fisher after this and explain why I didn't hunt him down to tell him he was going to be a father.

Then again, if he'd answered his phone or returned my call four months ago, he'd already know. I knew when I was leaving that night that he felt awkward. The sex had been off the charts, but I felt him pull away afterward, I just wasn't sure why. But I wasn't surprised when he didn't call after saying he would.

Either he can have nothing to do with my pregnancy or be a real father, but I'm done living in limbo.

By the time my shift finishes, I want to beg to stay longer just to avoid this conversation with Fisher. If only my feet weren't killing me and the hospital wasn't almost completely void of patients—somewhat unheard of in the ER when there's a full moon. I put on my coat and my purse crossways over my body, gearing up all my mental strength to walk out of here while at the same time hoping that Fisher fell asleep at home and forgot to come.

I greet the nurses coming on shift, happy to be among familiar faces, and scan my ID so the doors open to the waiting area. Fisher sits in a chair directly in front of the doors. His long legs are stretched out in front of him, ankles and arms crossed, eyes locked on mine.

"What? Did you set an alarm?" I slide through the doors before they shut.

He stands and runs his hand through his hair. "Let's go."

The man infuriates me with the way he's always so bossy. He still looks like a snack though. It's hard not to notice the fit body, the tattoos peeking out onto his hands and neck, and his beard that has a touch of gray here and there, though there's no gray to be found in his longish hair.

"Where are we going?" I ask.

"See you two later," Georgia says with an upbeat tone from her seat at the nurses' station. She's acting as though we're going on our first date instead of hashing out the details of our accidental pregnancy.

No, I didn't tell anyone that Fisher is the father, but anyone who works here knows the two of us had a budding friendship and spent time together.

"Bye, Georgia." I muster up a smile and wave.

Fisher grumbles a goodbye, and we head out of the hospital. The night air calms my tired body. After being in the hospital for twelve hours straight, I breathe the cool air in deeply.

"Want to hit the diner in Greywall?" I ask. We've gone on occasion since it's the only place around that's open twenty-four hours.

"We're going to my place."

I stop walking and he continues to his truck, not realizing I'm no longer next to him.

"I'm not going to your house." That's the scene of the crime.

He sighs and circles to face me, then puts his hands on

his hips as though I'm exhausting. "Why? It's quiet and we can talk without people overhearing us."

I roll my eyes. "First of all, who in Greywall would care about our lives? Plus, I don't know anyone there, do you?"

He points at the badge on the left side of his shirt.

Okay, so he has a point.

The fact that he's still in his uniform signals that he must have waited here the entire duration of my shift. Did he think I was going to abandon work halfway through just to avoid him?

"Fine, but I'm only staying for an hour." I'm not yet used to being back to shift work and I need my sleep.

His lips tip up in a smile, but it's not there long enough for me to fully appreciate it. It never is.

"I'll drive you there and back." He opens his passenger door.

I look at his big truck that makes my SUV look like a Tonka toy. "Did you hunt down my car to park beside me?"

"Easier to make sure you got to your car safely."

"You mean easier for you to swindle me into riding with you." I toss my bag in the back seat of my SUV and shut the door. "What's your game plan here, Fisher?"

"Game plan?" His poker face is in place as he stands outside the open passenger door. "I'm simply offering you a ride so you don't have to drive through the woods late at night."

Again, he has a point. His house is more remote than my apartment in Lake Starlight.

I blow out a breath. "I'm only riding with you so I can get home sooner and get to sleep." I use the handlebar to climb up into his truck, plopping down on the seat.

It's ridiculous that we're even meeting up at this hour, but we used to do it all the time after my shift at the hospital. I was always a bit wired and even if I went home, I couldn't sleep.

Fisher rounds the front of the truck and situates himself in the driver's seat. I forgot what a presence he has. Just watching his strong hand put the key in the ignition, turn down the radio, and pull the shifter down to reverse has me remembering the magic those long fingers are capable of.

I shake it off, ignoring the scent of his soap that lingers in the fibers of the fabric. I cannot allow myself to still be attracted to him after what he did to me.

Remember, Allie, he's no prince. He's the villain in your story.

He tossed my belief in true love into a meat grinder.

Thankfully, he doesn't say anything on the way to his house, so I use the time to mentally prepare my answers for all the questions he's sure to ask.

The house is dark, the driveway free of any cars or trucks. For the first time ever in his presence, I have an inkling of fear that maybe he doesn't want this baby, and I stupidly agreed to go back to his empty house in the middle of the night. He's the sheriff; surely he knows powerful people who can help him get away with murder.

"On second thought, maybe…"

"Get out of the car, Allie."

I pull out my phone. "Just so you know, I'm messaging Stella Bailey right now." I lean forward and squint at the house numbers hammered to the railing of his balcony. "I'm giving her the address. If you're planning anything crazy, she'll know."

He takes the key out of the ignition and stares at me. "What exactly do you think I'm gonna do?"

"Well, this is all a surprise to you. Maybe you want to kill me to get out of this situation."

"What?"

Yeah, his scrunched-up expression says I'm being all kinds of crazy. But you can never be too sure.

"It's happened before. Maybe you want us out of the way."

He mumbles something I can't make out and gets out of the truck, walking over to my side. The door opens and he's standing there with his hand out like a gentleman. A fake ass gentleman, because a gentleman would return a goddamn phone call.

"I'm not going to murder anyone." He reaches closer for me to accept his hand.

"Sheriffs aren't above the law." I slide my hand into his and step down from the truck to the driveway.

"Stop watching so many crime shows."

"I have people who would miss me."

That's semi true. Eventually my parents would figure it out when their weekly Sunday call went unanswered. Stella's perfect family keeps her busy, so it might take a few days for her to figure it out.

"The hospital!" I blurt out. They would notice when I didn't show up for my shift.

"Stop with this shit. I thought women just watched those Hallmark movies, but you seem to be obsessed with murder mysteries."

Investigation Discovery channel is my favorite, but I keep that to myself.

"I'm just putting it out there," I say, walking into his house first.

"I'll make us some tea," he says and goes into the kitchen.

"I never pegged you for a tea guy." I slide a chair out from the kitchen table and sit down so my back is facing the wall.

"I'm really not. Molly left some behind after they moved out."

"So you live here alone now?" I look around the place that doesn't appear to have been redecorated since he was a kid.

"Yeah." He glances over his shoulder. "It's just you and me here." He releases an evil laugh and I roll my eyes.

"You'd think with you being sheriff, you'd appreciate my abundance of caution."

He brings two cups over to the table and sets them down before folding himself into the chair across from me. "You got in the truck and you're here now." He raises his eyebrows.

Ugh, he's so damn annoying.

"Now, tell me why I'm just finding out you're carrying my baby?" He eyes my stomach, and all the joking gets pushed aside.

Time to face reality.

Chapter Three

Fisher

"For one, you could've answered your phone four months ago when I called." She sips her tea and diverts her eyes. That's one characteristic of Allie's that always grabbed the part of myself I try to ignore. She's so strong-willed and speaks her mind, but the minute she's vulnerable and turns shy, I want to shelter her, take care of her, and protect her.

"I was on a call and—"

She shakes her head. "Don't make excuses. I know why you didn't."

She actually doesn't, but I'm not ready to fill her in.

"I just—"

She cuts me off again. "You don't owe me anything, but don't be surprised now that I'm sitting here five months pregnant."

"You could have called me again. Or come by, or sent a letter, or something more than just one phone call. This is kind of important news."

She glances at her stomach and back at me with raised eyebrows. "I'm aware. I'm surprised you'd have wanted me to call when you don't want kids."

I probably told her that at one point during our friendship. I've never held back the fact marriage and kids aren't for me.

"Correct." Saying that while the woman carrying my child sits across from me feels wrong. "But now—"

"Nope." She shakes her head, interrupting me once again.

"Can I finish a sentence?" I push my tea away, standing to retrieve a beer from the fridge.

"I know what you're going to say. That this changes things."

"It does!" I twist the top of the bottle. "A helluva lot. You should've told me, Allie."

"I was going to. I tried, and when you didn't answer, I was going to call you again, but then... it was just a lot, okay? I needed to wrap my head around everything before I tried begging you to return a phone call."

My shoulders slump. I feel like an asshole. Hell, I was an asshole. "Well, this changes things."

"It doesn't have to. Listen, I don't want you half in. In means you're on board to be the best dad you can be. Which means joint custody or weekend visits. Visits you never miss."

I blow out a breath. I'm a sheriff. I can't always dictate when I'm needed.

"Within reason," she adds, confirming she knows what's going through my head. "But I don't want a ring. I don't want a relationship with you. I'm strictly talking about you being a dad. I will warn you though. Either you're one hundred percent in this or you're out. There's no room for in-between."

I down half my beer, my eyes glued to hers. Her straight back and eyes of steel show me how passionately she loves our baby already.

"I don't back away from my responsibilities. I don't remember the condom breaking, but I didn't exactly check it either." Lesson learned on that one.

"Again, Fisher, that isn't what I want to hear." She runs her hands over her stomach. "I'm not assuming you're going to get down on your knees and kiss my belly, but this isn't taking out the trash or doing the dishes. Babies need to be nurtured and cared for and most of all loved." She slides out of the chair, and I move to help her, but she quickly shoos me away. "I have to pee."

She goes to the half bath on this level, shutting the door behind her. I lower back down to my seat, twirling my beer bottle around on the table.

Me. A fucking father.

I've struggled to wrap my mind around it during her entire shift, but I can't visualize myself holding a baby, much less changing a diaper. I'm not the lovable guy. The one who wears his emotions for all to see. The one who would shower his son or daughter with love. That one scares me the most. But I meant what I said—I don't walk away from responsibilities. I'll figure it out.

The bathroom door opens behind me and she's so quiet I barely hear her walking across the floor. "Listen, maybe you should think this over. I don't need a decision now. We have a few months before the due date."

"Have you been to the doctor?"

"What? Of course." She takes her seat across from me.

"And?"

She looks a bit sheepish. "I haven't found out the gender, if that's what you're wondering. I'm not sure I want to know."

"Is the baby healthy?"

Her hesitance switches to an expression of annoyance. "Yes."

While she worked, I shuffled through all the scenarios for the remainder of her pregnancy, so I'm gonna throw out the most reasonable option. "Here's the plan. I think you should move in here."

"What?" Her voice raises.

"You don't have to stay in my room. There are three other bedrooms for you to choose from. Actually, you can have the master. I'll move out."

"Stop," she says, a panicked look in her eyes.

"And I'd like a list of your doctor appointments so I can plan to take off work."

She raises a hand. "Hold on, Fisher."

I finish my beer. "I'm all in."

She shakes her head and her gaze flickers to the table. "This is all too soon. You should sleep on it, think about it. And anyway, I can't move in here."

She stands and leaves the room, grabbing her purse on the way toward the door.

"Where are you going?"

"Crap!" she groans. "Can you please take me to my car?" She stands politely by the door, her hands clasped in front of her.

"Not until we finish talking. Why wouldn't you move in here?"

"Because..." She gives me the "you're crazy" eyes.

"It's closer to the hospital. I'll be here in the event that anything happens. Do you know how many times I find people who live alone?"

She throws her hands in the air. "I check in with my family every week. If I miss a shift at the hospital, someone would notice. Dori Bailey owns my apartment building, for goodness' sake. I can't overcook my noodles without her finding out about it. Not to mention, I've lived on my own for years."

"But not with my baby in your belly." I point at her stomach.

A long, languid breath flows out of her, but she immediately takes another deep breath as though she's in the middle of a hot yoga class. "This isn't how I planned all this."

I think she's talking more to herself than to me.

"I didn't plan it either." I step forward.

"Me living in the room right next to you?"

"You're welcome in my bed any night. Isn't there something about pregnancy hormones?" Nikki was all over Logan during her pregnancy.

She shakes her head, but a blush tinges her cheeks. "I do not want to sleep with the man I had a one-night stand with who didn't want to answer my calls."

I groan and my jaw clicks. "You knew the kind of guy I was before you slept with me. I made it clear that night."

"Believe me, I don't want anything from you, not even an orgasm."

"Just move in. After the birth, we can figure out a long-term solution. You'll save some money living here." I step closer, my body tense as if she's on the edge of a building about to jump and it's up to me to talk her down.

"No. Thank you, but no."

Her refusal to even consider the idea frustrates the hell out of me. "Why the fuck not?"

My chest tightens when I think about her alone in Lake Starlight. We were friends enough for me to know she has no family around here. And her best friend, Stella, has a huge plateful of her own responsibilities.

"Because."

My anger intensifies. "Why not?"

Her mouth opens and closes before she speaks. "This isn't how I pictured it as a little girl, you know?"

I take the purse from her shoulder, putting it on the table by the door. With my hand on her back, I lead her over to the couch. We need to discuss this and not with us standing six feet apart in an angry standoff.

"You mean you being pregnant?"

She sits down and I sit next to her. "I wanted the whole fairy tale."

"I don't think you want me as your husband."

A tear slips down her cheek, and I check the urge to swipe it away. "I wanted a man to love me with every piece of him so he couldn't imagine not having me in his life. We'd get married and eventually have kids that we planned to have, and we'd be so in love. I held out all these years for that to happen. But now I got knocked up by a tattooed sheriff who never wanted any kids and now I have to worry about custody and visitation and..." Sobs rack her body.

I lean in and gently tap her back to soothe her without really hugging her. "You can still have all that. Just after the baby is born."

"You don't even believe in love," she mumbles, and her head dives into my chest. "You don't do monogamy and you don't want kids."

The truth stings like the lash of a whip. I'm the worst person she could be tied to in this scenario. It doesn't mean I won't do my part though.

"I believe in love. Hell, my brothers and sisters keep dropping off because of what they call true love. It's just not for me. There are reasons why, but they don't matter. This isn't the early nineteen hundreds, Allie. You'll be able to find the love of your life even if you have a kid from another relationship."

"A one-night stand. It wasn't even a relationship." She sobs, her head falling into her hands in shame.

"Regardless, you'll still find your Mr. Right."

She sniffles and leans away from me, wiping her eyes. "Sorry."

"It's okay. I know pregnancy hormones are crazy."

She narrows her eyes at me. "I need to go home. Please take me to my car."

But I see the red-rimmed eyes and the bags under them. She looks exhausted.

"Just sleep here tonight."

She scoffs. "I'm not sleeping with you." Her hands press to the cushions and she stands, but I take her hand before she gets too far.

"You're exhausted. It's late. You can sleep in my bed, and I'll crash in Jed's old room."

Molly demanded a new bed, so he left his behind.

"I'm fine. I'm just a little tired. I was working in a private practice for months and I'm not used to the long shifts on my feet again yet."

I decide to try a different tactic. "It would save me from having to drive you to your car and then following you home."

She shakes her head like Rylan would do when he'd refuse to eat his vegetables as a kid. "You aren't my protector."

"Just stay."

I'm not sure what I say to convince her, but two minutes later, she relents. We head upstairs to my room, and I pull out a T-shirt and shorts for her to sleep in.

"Good night, Allie," I say, hovering by the door.

"Thank you. Good night."

We stand in awkward silence for a moment, but she heads into the master bathroom, so I leave the room.

I go to Jed's old room and sit on the edge of the bed, thinking about how different my life is about to be. It might be impulsive, but her moving in here is the right move. She shouldn't be living alone and pregnant. I'm closer to her work and she'll still have privacy while I'm working, but at the same time, my family lives pretty close. Should anything go wrong and I can't get to her, they can.

I stand and unbutton my shirt, taking it off and laying it over the chair Jed also left behind. Apparently Molly didn't want anything he screwed another girl on moving to the new place with them. It's then I realize I don't have shorts to sleep in. I hate sleeping in boxer briefs. They're way too restrictive. But with her in the house, sleeping naked like I normally would, feels weird.

I walk across the hall and rest my hand on the doorknob. I lightly tap, expecting her to probably be asleep by now. Her lack of an answer confirms my suspicion, so I slowly open the door and step in.

"Fisher!" she yells. She's walking out of the bathroom toward the bed where her clothes are laid out—and she's naked.

I freeze, staring at her body that's so different from the night we had sex. The belly I saw under her baggy clothes is so much more pronounced. Her tits are fuller, and damn if my dick doesn't harden with the thought of sliding between them and titty fucking her.

"Sorry," I mumble, still frozen.

"Get out!" she yells, grabbing the shirt and covering herself with it.

"Sorry again." I shut the door and place my forehead on it.

Damn, she's still fucking hot, and now I'm going to have to beat off to the thought of fucking her if I have any hope of getting some sleep. I just wish I didn't have to do it in Jed's bed.

Chapter Four

Allie

I cannot believe I put myself in this position.

Fisher is still sleeping, and I'm stranded at his house with no one to come and pick me up. I could call an Uber, but news travels way too fast in this town. Being picked up in the morning at Fisher Greene's house isn't going to be on the latest Scandals of Sunrise episode if I can help it.

I call the one person who might be a better option for me other than walking all the way back to the hospital.

"Well, well, well..." Kingston answers Stella's phone. "Have we told the bastard yet?"

Stella's husband, Kingston, is a firefighter, and he owns half the sports complex where most kids in the area go for sports. He also knows way more about my business than he should.

"Where's your lovely wife?" I ask.

"She's on diaper duty. You're in luck, you've got me." There's some kind of ruckus in the background. "Oh man, what did you do, Maven?"

"I take it you're on toddler duty while she's on baby duty?"

I'm envious of the way Kingston and Stella juggle their kids, especially with a newborn in the mix.

"She has something I don't have to help out in that department." He laughs, and Maven's cries begin in the background. "Oh crap. Hold on. It's okay, sweetie. Mistakes happen. Spills happen."

She continues to sob.

"Let me get Stella, I have to calm down my perfectionist daughter." He groans, getting up from what I expect is the floor of Maven's toy room. "Stell?"

"Shh... she's finally down," Stella says.

"Down? She can't fall asleep. I have an important day of errands today and I need her to sleep during them," Kingston says. I think he covered the phone, but I can hear him anyway.

"You can't make infants sleep when you want them to," Stella says.

The muffling sound stops before he says to me, "Here. Let me know if I have to beat anyone up. I know he's the sheriff, but I know people."

Then I hear a kiss between them. Two seconds later, a door shuts and there's no more Maven crying.

"I saw your text from the middle of the night. So?" Stella whispers like we're about to gossip about our latest Netflix binge.

"My life is not a soap opera."

"Actually, Allie, it kind of is right now."

I sit on his couch and glance at the stairway. Still not one peep coming from upstairs. Covering my mouth, I whisper, "I'm still at his house. I spent the night."

Dead silence.

"I didn't sleep with him!"

"Oh. Phew." A long breath flows over the line as though we were in a life-and-death situation. "You scared me."

"Thanks for the vote of confidence." I rise from the

couch, needing anything to get rid of the gnawing in my stomach.

"Why would you stay there?"

"By the time we were done talking, it was really late and I was tired and—"

"Uh-huh, keep the excuses coming."

I open the fridge to find beef jerky, a few eggs, and not one vegetable in sight. Taking the bag of beef jerky, I go back to the family room, stopping to listen for a moment at the stairs.

Still no sound.

"They're not excuses. Three a.m. is a perfectly reasonable time to have a deep conversation when you work the shifts we do." I tear a piece of jerky with my teeth. Surprisingly, it's not that bad.

"I am a doctor. I get late phone calls." I hear some noise in the background.

"Are you doing your makeup?"

"Multitasking is my life." She chuckles. "I still have to do Maven's hair."

"You mean Kingston can't handle that?" The man is perfection. I would've thought he could style his daughter's hair.

"He thinks he can, but he can't. He's learning though, so maybe after Maisey, he'll have it down pat." We both laugh. "Stop trying to change the subject. So he knows everything now, right?"

I snap off another piece of jerky and look around the room as if I'm a kid being interrogated by the police because I stole a pair of earrings.

"Allie." She uses her challenging tone. She assumes I haven't told him the whole truth, and well... she knows me. She's right.

"Almost everything," I mumble around a mouthful of jerky. I turn the bag over to read the nutritional facts because how have I never tried this delicious dried meat before?

"I'm pretty sure the part you left out could possibly be a game changer, or at the very least a holy shit moment." A door opens and Stella says, "Come here, Mave, let's do your hair."

"I was already in shock. I wasn't prepared to see him last night, okay? And then he practically kidnapped me and told me to spend the night. I like to take things slow."

She laughs so loudly I pull the phone away from my ear.

"Be nice, okay? Let's remember you and Kingston early on." They were in love but tortured themselves for years by staying apart. The giddy fairy tale believer in me says it was fate that brought them back together.

"We took it slow."

"Just because I'm knocked up by the man doesn't mean…" I stop talking and she giggles again, knowing her point was made. "Yeah, okay, but he might not be prepared for this news."

"I'm pretty sure after the first news, not much else is going to surprise him." Maven whines in the background. "Hold still, baby girl."

Stella can say it isn't a big deal because she's never heard that news herself, but I took it hard when the doctor told me. It changes so much. Which is why I'm currently sitting in my clothes from yesterday, eating beef jerky on my baby daddy's couch. In truth, I'm kind of lost in my life, which I blame on my horrible decision to stay here last night.

"I know you're a true believer of soul mates and fate and serendipity and all that, but no one said this can't turn out differently than you think it will. I mean, look at Kingston's brother, Denver. He wasn't much of a commitment guy, and now he's married with kids. Actually!" The excitement in her voice makes me groan because I know exactly where her thoughts are going.

"Thanks, but no."

"Come on. I'm sure him and Cleo—"

"No. I'll tell Fisher today when he drops me off at my car."

"That makes it sound like you had a booty call last night," she jokes.

"Booty," Maven says in the background.

"Ignore me," Stella says to her daughter.

"Are you teaching our daughter bad words?" Kingston's voice sounds faint.

"Talk to your husband. I'm gonna go," I say. She's clearly busy. I'm not going to ask her to come get me.

"Tell him, Allie," Stella says.

"I'll tell him. Let it go."

"Tell me what?"

My head whips around to see Fisher standing there in a pair of shorts and no shirt. His longer dark hair is messy, and his olive skin is sprinkled with tattoos. Don't get me started on the thick scruff on his face. The sight of him has my jaw hanging like a monkey off a tree. Seriously, what god made this guy?

"Gotta go. I'll talk to you later." I hang up on Stella and Kingston laughing as if my life is a joke. Which, at the moment, it kind of is. Especially from their perfect snow globe.

Fisher sits next to me on the couch, stealing the bag of beef jerky. Suddenly, I feel like I'm in high school, about to tell my crush I like him. He took the news about the pregnancy well; surely this will go fine too.

"So?" He uses his teeth to snap off a piece of beef jerky. "Sorry the fridge is so empty, it's been a week from hell, but let me take you out to eat. We can go to Two Brothers and an Egg. I heard they have some killer muffins."

A muffin sounds great right about now. Then I imagine some pancakes and eggs and my stomach rumbles—more because I have to feed my growing baby, then myself, of course. "Sure."

"Wanna tell me who you were talking to and what you're keeping from me?" He leans forward and rests his forearms on his thighs, staring at me over his shoulder with a softness to his eyes that makes me want to blurt it out.

"Can we eat first?" I ask like the wimp I am.

He smirks and shakes his head with a sweet smile. A smile that says he trusts I'll spill the details in due time. "Sure, I'll give you a reprieve. Especially since you let me sleep in and I only had jerky to offer you and our baby for breakfast."

My insides go to mush with his word choice of *our* baby.

"You care if I take a shower? I have to be at the station at noon."

I shake my head. "Go ahead."

He rises off the couch, and I can't help but admire his perfect form. The V of his torso, the sprinkling of dark hair that teasingly travels under the waistband of his shorts. "Keep looking at me like that and I'm gonna drag you into the shower with me."

I snap my eyes up to meet his smoldering gaze and my insides quake.

"Sorry, I was just dazed," I say, waving him off.

He nods with a humorous smile before heading upstairs. For a moment, I swear his white teeth sparkled like in those fairy tales. The ones where a prince saves the damsel from the tower. People think I should want a prince to rescue me. Fisher wanting me to move in so he can look after me because I'm pregnant is an admirable quality, but I'm fully capable of handling myself. It's love I've always searched for, not a protector.

I lean back on the couch, remembering my grandpa on his knees at my grandma's bedside. The words that poured out of him, how he gripped her hand, the kisses he kept casting over her as though he was afraid someone was going to wheel her away. You wouldn't expect it from his tough war veteran exterior, but he always doted on my grandma and wanted nothing more than to make her happy. His undying love for my grandma resonated with me and instilled within me the belief that there are soul mates in this world. And if you're lucky, you find them.

Fisher is lightning fast getting ready, and the ends of his hair are still damp from the shower when he returns downstairs. He's in his uniform, which I should've known he'd be, but I can't help gawking because he looks so good in it. Trying to avoid blatantly staring at him, I grab my purse and prepare to leave.

"Ready?" he asks, grabbing his keys off the table by the front door and opening it for me.

"Yeah."

I wait for him to lock up before we descend the steps to the driveway. His hand lands on my elbow and I stop and stare at him.

"I'm helping you."

"I'm pregnant, Fisher, not geriatric."

"Exactly, and if you fall, it could harm our baby."

I hold back a cringe at his sentence. I don't want to start an argument right before I tell him the rest of my news, so I allow him to guide me as if there's ice on the stairs and I'm Ethel or Dori.

His hovering continues until we reach the truck. He tells me to change the way my seat belt lays over my belly, and he wants to drop me off at the doors while he finds a parking spot. By the time he meets me in the diner, I'm already salivating over the food I've stalked on the dishes delivered to nearby tables.

The minute he walks in, people greet him with handshakes and waves.

Tad, the owner, follows Fisher with a cup of coffee and sets it down once Fisher slides into the chair across from me. I asked for one of the two tables since it's becoming more difficult to fit in a booth. Good times.

"Thanks, Tad. This is Allie." Fisher holds his hand out to me.

"Hey, Allie, what can I get you? Tea? Juice?"

"I'll have orange juice, and can you bring me one of those muffins before we order please?"

He smiles like he knew I'd ask for one. "Which kind? We have blueberry, morning glory, and cinnamon streusel today."

"Morning glory. Thank you." I rub my belly like he didn't notice I'm pregnant, but it's my way of excusing the obvious urgency in my voice. The beef jerky just didn't do it for me.

"Hungry, huh?" Fisher asks, not touching his coffee.

"Starving, actually."

Tad returns, muffin in hand, with a speed that impresses me. He knows how to take care of a pregnant woman. Feed her fast and she's happy. Over his shoulder, I notice some people looking over and whispering.

Leaning forward, I say in a low voice to Fisher, "People are staring."

Fisher doesn't bother to glance over his shoulder. He only nods. "It's Sunrise Bay. I'm the sheriff and you're pregnant. People will speculate."

"But…" I do not want to be fodder for all the chatter in this town. But when he mentioned food, it was as if all the other thoughts went out of my brain. "Right, small town and all that."

He glances at my untouched muffin. "So, are you ready?"

He sips his coffee once I bite my muffin, which is pure sweet bliss. I want to shove it all in my mouth and yell to Tad to keep 'em coming. But I maintain my dignity—barely.

"Um…"

"Ready to order?" Based on his stellar timing, Tad is my new favorite guy. Purveyor of muffins and interruptions. Heavy tip coming for him.

We both order, and while I feel as if I order the entire menu, Fisher orders an omelet and fruit.

"Fruit?" I ask.

"Yeah." He shrugs.

"No bacon or sausage or hash browns?"

He chuckles. "How do you think I keep this body you keep drooling over?"

My eyes narrow. "I am not drooling."

He shrugs as though he doesn't care either way.

"Time's up. I've been patient. Reward me." He looks at me expectantly.

I stare at him for a moment, then look around the room. Maybe it's best that we're here. If this goes south, at least I have an endless food supply to drown my sorrows. "About the baby…"

He straightens in his seat. "Is there something wrong?"

I shake my head. "No, but—"

"He or she is healthy? You said everything was fine."

I nod. "It is. But the thing is—"

"Are you worried that I want to find out the sex? I'm cool if you don't want to. I mean, I'm flexible."

"We can discuss that later. I have an ultrasound this week."

"Perfect." He pulls out his phone. "What day and time? I'll make sure I'm available to take you."

I shake my head, but he waits expectantly for me to answer, so I go from memory. "Wednesday at eleven."

He buries his head in his phone, his thumbs typing away. "Why were you so nervous about telling me that?" He grabs my hand. "I know this is weird, but I'll totally respect your privacy during the exams and stuff. And don't worry, during the delivery, I won't even think about going south, okay? But I would like to be in there if that's okay?"

I never thought Fisher would want to be so involved, and I curse myself for the way my heartbeat picks up speed at his words. I thought for sure he'd be scared, he'd retreat, he'd demand a paternity test. But he's accepting and wants to be part of it all.

"Here you go, guys." Tad returns to our table with our food. "I had Brad put your order ahead of the others. The sheriff has important business, and I'm not about to make a pregnant woman wait for food."

Definitely a favorite. I smile at him. "Thank you so much."

He nods and walks away.

Fisher opens his silverware and places the napkin on his lap, digging into his meal.

He thinks that's what I had to tell him, so what's the harm in waiting a little longer? I place my own napkin on my lap and eat.

I'll tell him... eventually.

Fisher

On the way from the diner to Sunrise Bay's sheriff's office, I turn on the radio to try to get my mind to stop spinning. All the worries and uncertainties are like a damn merry-go-round constantly circling inside my head. I've never done well with uncertainty. I prefer my personal life to be on an even keel and steady, but the sheriff side of me likes to prepare for the unexpected.

As soon as I turn up the volume, my stepsister Nikki's voice rings in my ears. "So yes, Sunrise Bayers, my step-brother, Fisher Greene, our town sheriff, is going to be a daddy."

"Fuck!"

Damn her and her stupid gossip show.

I reach for the radio to turn it off, but think better of it. I need to be prepared for any questions that come my way now that our entire small town knows my business.

And how the hell did Nikki find out this fast anyway?

"Do you think it'll come out with an armful of tattoos?" her cohost, Chip, chimes in.

I still can't believe her sidekick is a man in his fifties with the personality of sandpaper.

"Hey now, that baby is my future niece or nephew."

"Well, you'll be happy to know it was well fed this morning, from what I heard," Chip says.

"Don't shame a pregnant woman, Chip. You grow a human being from scratch and tell me you don't need an extra muffin… or two."

I cross my fingers that the conversation turns to Nikki and Chip at odds, so they'll leave Allie and me the hell out of it.

"I'm just saying she took a half dozen muffins home. At least that's what I heard."

"She can eat everything in the diner. She's pregnant and eating for two. I know you're a bachelor, but have you really never heard these phrases before?"

Chip grumbles something unintelligible.

"Back to us having a little boy or girl join the Greene clan. I'm so excited for Noah to have a baby cousin. And they won't be too far apart in age either."

"They'll be, like, a year apart," Chip says.

"Um, no. Weren't you listening to my report? Sources say she's about five months along. Which means the baby will be here right after the holidays." The excitement in Nikki's voice pulls a reluctant smile out of me.

A baby in only a few months.

"Why did she wait so long to tell him?" Chip asks the pointed question.

The question I wanted an answer to. The same question Allie had a good excuse for. I never returned her phone call. She was scared. Had she left me a voice mail and told me she was pregnant, I guarantee I would have called.

"Knowing Fisher, he dodged her after they slept together."

Nikki's words are a quick slash to the heart. Mostly because they ring true.

"He isn't exactly marriage material."

God, can Chip just shut the fuck up? I press harder on the accelerator.

"Let me just say, I've done the math, and I'm pretty sure that around the time Allie would've gotten pregnant, my grandma Ethel and her friend Dori were on their typical fix-up mission at our annual summer bash."

"Ethel's not actually your grandma," Chip says.

I shake my head because one day Nikki is going to lose her shit and go ballistic on Chip in the studio, and no strings I can pull will help her. The entire town will have overheard her committing murder.

"She *is* my grandma. Maybe not by blood, but I love her like a grandma. Jeez, Chip, you're awfully chatty this morning. If this keeps up, I'm taking away your coffee privileges at The Grind."

"You can't do that." He sounds like a temperamental two-year-old.

"Zoe is a dear friend, and let's remember she dates my husband's trainer."

"Former trainer," Chip says.

I choke out a laugh as though Nikki's in front of me and I'm in danger of catching her wrath if she sees me laughing.

"Chip!" she shouts. "My hormones still aren't all back to normal."

"What does that mean?"

"It means I can strangle you to death and have an excuse."

The phone in the studio starts ringing, and I shake my head, listening to the chaos of her morning show. She'll probably be asking for a bottle of vodka in a minute. But I can't feel too bad given that Nikki's outed me before I've even had a chance to speak to anyone in my family, let alone figure shit out with Allie.

"Why are you patching a call through, Matt?" Nikki asks. There's a pause and Nikki grunts. "Hi, Ethel."

"Dori's here too," the other woman says.

"Hi, Dori," Nikki says with a groan.

"I just want to say thank you. I'm all teary-eyed over here with your words about loving me like a grandma," Grandma says.

Nikki sighs. "I do."

"I do too." Grandma sniffles.

What a shit show.

"Now, Chip, I'd be looking over your shoulder from now on. Where do you get off saying Nikki's not my granddaughter?"

"Ethel... I—"

"No excuses. Watch yourself. We have canes and tennis balls under our walkers. You never know, one of us might just go a little crazy one of these days." There's no levity in her voice because Grandma is always on the defensive when it comes to her grandchildren, step included.

"Oh, come on," Chip whines.

"You should be happy I don't take you over my knee," Ethel says, and Dori laughs in the background.

"I have to finish the show now," Nikki interrupts Grandma's threat.

"Okay, sweetie, good job on the news."

"Fisher might be mad," Nikki says, sounding concerned.

"Then he should have kept it zipped up."

I feel a rush of heat to my cheeks. My grandma, thinking about me having sex, sends a shiver down my spine.

Nikki laughs. "Very true. Bye, ladies."

They each say goodbye, and if there is a god, this means the segment is over.

"Now, what was I saying…" Nikki trails off. "Oh yes, so at the barbecue, Ethel and Dori brought Allie to try to fix her up with Jed or Cam."

"Cameron Baker?" Chip asks with a laugh.

"I know, right? But they had good intentions. They didn't know then that Jed was messing around with my BFF. But Fisher resembled a dog protecting his bowl the minute Allie showed up. He didn't like the idea of her being fixed up with one of his brothers or his best friend."

"Interesting. So you think Allie might be the one? But he didn't answer her phone call for five months, right?"

"Rumor has it. But from what I know about Allie, I'm not sure she'd chase him down. Besides, she ran away too. She left the hospital and went to work in Lake Starlight, which I bet is no coincidence. It tells me that Fisher must've hurt her."

Maybe Nikki should put her talents for digging up intel to work for the FBI.

"He'll have to grovel," Chip says.

I inhale deeply, hoping to relieve some of the guilt weighing heavy in my heart.

"Well, if Fisher wants Allie, he better put his ego aside."

"Then again, he might not care."

I sip the to-go cup of coffee Tad gave me. I'm going to need the extra dose of caffeine to get me through today because I slept like shit last night, even if Allie did let me sleep in.

"No man who doesn't care waits until three in the morning to talk to a woman and takes her back to his place. Believe me, folks, I know a lot of you feel as though our sheriff doesn't have it in him, but I call bullshit. I bet Fisher is married before year's end."

The coffee sprays out of my mouth all over the inside of my windshield. "Damn it!"

"I'll take the bet," Chip says, and now I want to strangle Chip again.

I shut off the radio, not wanting to know anything else they have to say.

Once I'm parked in the parking lot of the Sunrise Bay Sheriff's Office, I open my glove compartment to grab some napkins to clean up the mess. All it does is smear all over the glass.

"Fucking hell." I open up the truck door, grab my coffee, and slam it shut.

The second I open the door of the office, Lilian greets me with a smile and a blush that makes me think she spotted me through the window and just ran back to her desk after gossiping about me with our coworkers.

"Lilian," I say, nodding and walking by her.

"Mornin', Sheriff Greene."

I walk past the few desks to my office, ignoring everyone murmuring hello because they're too afraid to make eye contact with me. I'm not an idiot. I know Nikki's radio station was just playing in here. It is every day.

By the time I reach my office, I want to hurl my coffee at the damn door. I flop down in my chair as my cell phone rings. I pull it out of my pocket and see Cade's name on the screen. Of course my older brother wants to check up on me. The poor guy's been trying to make sure we're all okay since our mom died.

A knock on the door stops me from answering the call.

"Come in," I say in the gruff tone most are used to with me.

"Good mornin'." Mato comes into my office and sits in the chair across from my desk.

"What? Nothing to say?"

A smile betrays his usual stoic expression, and he raises both hands. "I don't meddle."

"Bullshit." I sip my coffee now that I've calmed down slightly.

"You obviously don't wanna talk about it. I heard the news this morning before Nikki's show anyway."

I roll my eyes. "How?"

He quirks one dark eyebrow to suggest I'm a moron for forgetting what our small town is like. "There was an accident out on the Glenn Highway in the early a.m. Had to question some people at the hospital."

I groan. Of course. The hospital. It's worse than the TMZ newsroom. "What are they saying?"

He rests his ankle on his other knee and leans back in the chair. "That Allie surprised you with the pregnancy. There are rumors that the baby isn't yours, all the way to she's expecting triplets because she's so big already. You know how it is." He shrugs as though it's no big deal.

I don't say anything. Triplets? Fuck. I try to remember how big Nikki was at this point in her pregnancy, because Allie's stomach isn't gigantic, but she was pretty thin before. How the hell do I know what one pregnant belly looks like compared to another one?

"So?" he interrupts my thoughts.

"What?"

"Is it yours?"

"As far as I know. I never asked for a paternity test."

He laughs and bends forward, continuing to laugh at my expense. "Classic."

My eyes narrow. "What?"

"You went all protective. Probably started pounding your chest. Go back to my jungle." He lifts his fisted hands and pounds his chest, mimicking King Kong.

"What the hell are you talking about?"

He grows somber for a moment, but from the smile that won't vanish, he's holding in his laugh by a breath. "You took her to your house. People have pictures of your hand on the small of her back. Didn't you listen to Nikki's segment this morning?"

"I tuned in late." Now I wish I'd heard it all.

"Someone reported that you pulled her into the room where your niece was being treated, then you waited outside the emergency room doors until three in the morning."

"I got dinner at the cafeteria," I grumble, shaking my head in annoyance.

"Then you two had breakfast and she was wearing the same clothes as yesterday. At this point, people are fairly sure you're a couple."

I squeeze my coffee. "We're not."

"But you are having a baby together?" He locks his eyes with mine.

"We are."

"Say it," he goads me.

"You're ridiculous. What did you come in here to talk about—other than my personal life?"

"We just received an interesting call."

"What is it?"

"Someone called to say someone broke into their Netflix account."

"Tell them to call Netflix then." I push the button to fire up my computer.

He shakes his head, another smile tipping his lips. "They're suggesting that someone broke in, watched a bunch of shows they normally wouldn't watch, and now all their recommendations are all wrong."

"You're kidding me, right?" I push a hand through my hair.

He shakes his head. "Afraid not."

I stand and take another sip of my coffee before dumping the cup in the trash. "Let's go. Where to?"

"George Lehman's."

Of course, it couldn't be anyone other than the leader of the Sunrise Bay Gossip Brigade.

Chapter Six

Allie

*L*ater that week, I'm in the waiting room of Stella's practice, my foot tapping on the carpet. The sound of the waterfall feature she had installed on one wall is doing nothing to soothe my nerves. All it's doing is making me have to pee.

I've managed to dodge Fisher since our breakfast, needing a little space. Sure, he knows secret number one, but there's still a big one for him to find out, and I'm nervous about how he'll react. That's if he even shows up for this ultrasound appointment. When we parted ways at the diner, he said he would no matter what, but the gossip around the hospital is that someone is breaking into elderly people's houses and messing with their Netflix accounts. Knowing Fisher, he won't rest until he finds whoever is responsible. Which has worked out well for me since he hasn't had time to push me to move in or even ask more questions about the pregnancy. But if he shows up today, he'll find out what I've been keeping from him.

I glance at the clock. My appointment time was ten minutes ago. I imagine myself storming up to Cindy, the receptionist, and telling her to get me in a room and if a hot sheriff shows up asking for me, tell him she doesn't know who I am.

But that'd be taking the easy way out. The news will be like a bomb drop and there's no way to stop it from exploding and spraying us both with shrapnel.

"Allie?" Heather comes out behind the closed door with my file in her hand.

I spring out of my chair as if I'm not five months pregnant and about to lose all bladder control. I greet her and walk toward the doorway as fast as I can.

"Hold up," a deep voice rings out across the room.

A long breath flows out of my mouth as my head lowers until my chin is tucked to my chest. I was so close.

The waiting room quiets—probably because most of the women are watching Fisher. I peek over my shoulder. Sure enough, he's in his uniform but without his hat, so his dark, wavy hair is tousled to perfection. A memory surfaces of my fingers running through those dark, soft strands every time he thrust inside me.

"Sorry I'm late," he says.

"And you are?" Heather asks, her voice razor sharp with protectiveness.

"I'm with Allie." He disregards her and looks at me. "Sorry, got hung up at work."

"Another case of the Netflix hijacker?"

He rolls his eyes and nods.

"Okay then, follow me." Heather leads us down the hallway to the farthest room. The one where she does the ultrasounds.

Fisher's footsteps behind me sound like a doomsday premonition, and I take a deep breath. This is the other reason I hadn't yet worked up the nerve to tell him about the pregnancy. But we're here now and the reveal is inevitable.

Fellow nurses watch us, whispering to one another like old church ladies. I lift my hand, saying hello to ex-coworkers, but none of them are focused on me. They're fixated on Fisher as though he's the latest Hollywood heartthrob.

Don't they know Gavin Price is still in town?

All three of us step into the room, and I set my purse on one of the chairs.

Heather arranges a couple of things on the counter and says over her shoulder, "Stella wants to check you today with it being five months and—"

"That's fine. Fisher can step out while I change."

She chuckles. "I'll take you to an exam room after the ultrasound. I don't need you to change for this, silly. What's up with you?"

Pregnancy brain mixed with a good dose of nerves, I want to tell her, but instead I smile.

I slide up on the table while Heather prepares the ultrasound machine. She tucks towels under the waistband of my pants, then walks across the room to turn off the lights. Fisher's examining the room as if he's just entered a crime scene, taking in every little item.

"Fisher," I whisper.

He inches closer, sliding his hand into mine. "This is what I'm supposed to do, right? It isn't going to hurt, is it?"

I stare into dark eyes that are so full of kindness and concern. He really is a good guy, even if he didn't choose this situation for himself.

"Okay, you know the drill." Heather squirts the gel on my stomach.

Fisher's eyes tear away from mine to watch what Heather's doing, but I can't look away from him. He watches with intent and intrigue as though he's memorizing her steps. Either that or he's still wowed by the sight of my stomach. I saw the way he reacted to it the night he barged into his room and I was naked.

"Will we hear the heartbeat?" he asks.

"Yes, that's why Allie has to have so many ultrasounds. The Doppler wouldn't be effective."

Lucky for me, Fisher doesn't ask any more questions and probably has no idea what the Doppler is.

"Here's a little one," Heather says, and Fisher and I concentrate on the screen. "Do you want to know the sex?"

A knock sounds on the door and it creaks open. Stella walks in. "I didn't miss it, did I?"

Her hair is down and curly today, a stark contrast to her white coat. As usual, Stella's makeup is flawless on her umber skin and I have no idea how she does it when my mascara looks like a ten-year-old was playing in her mom's makeup bag.

She puts her hand out to Fisher, completely unfazed. "Oh, hi, Fisher. I wasn't sure you'd be joining us today."

He nods and shakes her hand. "Yes. Nice to see you again, Dr. Bailey."

She shoos him away with her perfectly manicured nails. I want to come back as Stella Bailey in my next life. "Call me Stella." She squeezes my ankle. "How are things?"

Stella studies me, rounding the bed. Her question isn't about how I'm doing, I can tell. It's more... has this big man gone crazy yet with all the surprises I've sprung on him? So I dodge her eye contact. I haven't told Fisher yet and I'm not sure what his reaction will be.

"I was just asking them if they wanted to know the sex. This little one is spread wide open."

Stella peeks over Heather's shoulder and smiles. "Well?" She looks at both of us.

Fisher squeezes my hand to grab my attention. "Whatever you want."

I nod for Heather to tell us, knowing I'll never be able to wait.

Her white teeth glow in the dim room. "It's a girl," she says with a big smile.

"A girl?" Fisher says in what I think might be disbelief.

"Is that okay?" I ask, because he could be one of those stupid macho men who only wants boys.

"She's healthy?" He ignores me and sets his eyes on Heather. "Ten fingers, ten toes?"

Stella looks at the pictures Heather took. "She looks great." She places her hand on my knee. "She looks perfect."

I'm so lost in the moment of finding out that I'm having a girl, a tear slips down my cheek, then another one topples over, chasing the first one like siblings racing after each other. Fisher's thumb brushes away my tears and our eyes lock.

We're going to be parents. This is real.

"Just one more," Heather says and moves the wand to the other side of my stomach.

I'm still basking in knowing I'm going to be the mother of a daughter, so I don't react, but Fisher catches what she says and watches Heather move to the other side. "Wait. What?"

"Jesus, Allie," Stella scolds in a hushed tone, rounding the end of the bed.

"The other baby. Baby A is a girl. Now let's see if she's going to have a sister or a brother." Heather's all upbeat as if this is her first time doing an ultrasound for twins. In the age of fertility treatments, I can't imagine that it would be.

"Twins?" Fisher's face drains of color and his eyes snap to mine. This time, the kindness is replaced with questions.

My mouth dries out completely, leaving my only option as a nod.

"Twins?" He looks back over at Stella and Heather. I'm not even sure what they say, but his olive complexion turns even more pale, and he says, "Two," over and over until he sways and tips to the side.

"Whoa!" Stella rushes over and they both collapse to the floor, Stella taking a lot of Fisher's weight so he doesn't bash his head. "Seriously, Allie, this is a better option? For him to find out this way? Heather, get me some smelling salts."

Heather sets the wand in the holder on the side of the machine and rushes over to a drawer. Fisher isn't the first father to be to faint, but it usually happens during birth. If Fisher is passing out from just the news of having twins, I'm not sure he'll last through the delivery.

I struggle to sit up on my own, but manage and look at the floor. Fisher blinks a few times, his head in Stella's lap.

The door opens without anyone knocking and a cloud of blue and white hair peeks in. Ethel and Dori.

"Oh, we thought we missed it." Ethel stares at her grandson. "Stop being such a wimp. You're a sheriff, for Pete's sake."

He sits up and rests his arms on his bent knees, his head tilted down between them. Stella gets up off the floor, giving me a look usually reserved for Kingston when she's mad at him.

"Are you okay, Fisher? I know it's a shock," Stella says.

"What's a shock? Is something wrong with the baby?" Dori asks.

"Dori, Ethel, you need to leave. I'm not even going to ask who let you in." Stella puts her hand on both of their backs and ushers them toward the door.

"We brought donuts from Sweet Suga Things," Dori says proudly, as though she's got Willy Wonka's golden ticket.

"Thank you, but they still shouldn't let you back here."

It's clear Stella's going to be talking to some of the staff once she leaves this room. Not sure how much it will help though.

"Fisher's my grandson," Ethel argues over her shoulder. "I'm the great-grandmother."

"And if Fisher decides to tell you, that's up to him." Stella's tone brokers no argument.

"Come on, Allie, we're friends," Dori complains, her feet sliding closer to the door. "We're old. You need to treat your elders with respect."

"And you need to give Allie and Fisher some privacy."

Man, I have such a lady crush on Stella right now. The way she can always handle Dori and Ethel is beyond impressive. Both of the old women groan, but Stella shuts the door in their complaining faces.

"You're so good with them," I say with a huge smile, but Stella doesn't even look at me.

She puts her hand out to Fisher. "Let's get you up slowly."

Fisher accepts her hand, pushing up off the floor. I'd bet if he didn't have the amount of scruff he does, his cheeks would be tinged pink with embarrassment. "I'm fine."

"Do you two need a moment?" Stella asks, but she's only looking at Fisher, so I guess it's only his decision. I'm on the shit list.

"No." He shakes his head. "I apologize. I just—"

Stella touches his arm. "It happens a lot. Especially when you're in shock." She cuts a mean look my way.

He comes over to my side.

Heather gets herself set back up, straightens her back, and squirts more gel on my stomach. "Okay, let's find baby B."

She scans my stomach and I watch her take pictures.

The tension in the room is thick, and I can't help but think that everyone is mad at me. But when Heather turns on the sound to listen to the heartbeat, the thick fog of tension disperses as though the sun's just come up. Tears prick my eyes again.

Fisher slides his hand into mine. I look over to find him staring at the screen. "And?"

Heather turns to Stella. "You can tell them this time."

Stella finally makes eye contact with me again. I knew her grudge wouldn't last long. "Baby B is a boy. You're having a girl and a boy."

I close my eyes, feeling blessed beyond measure.

The door opens without warning and Dori pokes her head in. "Stella?"

Stella shakes her head and heads over to the door. "Congratulations, you two. I'll see you in the exam room." She slides out of the room to talk to Dori.

"Okay, I'm going to give you two a moment." Heather passes me a towel. "Use this to wipe off, and once you're done, I'll be waiting in the hallway."

"Thanks, Heather." I sit up with the help of her and Fisher. I cannot even imagine what this will be like the bigger I get.

The door shuts and Fisher sets his gaze on me. "Was this the news you needed to tell me?"

I nod and press my lips together.

"You didn't think I'd need to know we're having twins?"

"I tried, but—"

He cuts me off. "Allie, this is never gonna work unless you're completely up front with me."

I climb down from the table and drop the towel in the designated bin, lowering my shirt over my stomach. "I know, but I was scared."

"Why? Did you think I was going to get mad? It's not under your control that you're having twins." He runs his fingers through his hair, and I hate that everything down south stirs.

"I know, but still."

"What's going on in that head of yours?" He comes up to me and places his finger under my chin, tilting my face to look at him.

"I just thought maybe it would scare you even more and you'd…"

"Allie, I told you—I'm in."

I nod, tears stinging my eyes. "Okay."

There's still a layer of doubt under his words. He didn't want this life, didn't choose it, and I fear that one day he's going to realize I'm bringing him down. I can't bear the idea of my children ever feeling unwanted.

He brings his hands to rest on my upper arms and ducks down a bit so we're at the same eye level. "Let's go to dinner tonight and really talk this out."

"Okay," I say meekly. "I'm sorry. I should've told you right away."

"Apology accepted, although it's embarrassing as hell that your best friend had to catch me before I hit the floor."

I shrug. "She's a doctor."

"And I'm a sheriff."

I chuckle and head over to the door. When I open it, I find Ethel and Dori waiting in the hallway on a bench. They both stand when they see us.

"So?" Ethel says, peeking over my shoulder as though the empty room behind me holds all the answers.

"Go home, Grandma. Everything is good." Fisher puts his hand on the small of my back, leading me to follow Heather.

"You guys are buzzkills. I might just take you out of my will, Fisher Greene," Ethel calls to our backs.

"You can tell them," I say in a low voice when we get in the room.

"Hell no. The whole town will know then. We'll decide when to tell them ourselves. We're a team." He looks intently at me, waiting for me to agree.

"Go team." I raise my arm in a fist pump with about the same amount of enthusiasm as if I was cheering on my worst enemy.

Chapter Seven

Fisher

The exam room isn't nearly as inviting as the ultrasound room. It's stark white and sterile.

"So go ahead and change. She'll be in soon." Heather places a gown on the table.

"Can I have a bodyguard at the door?" Allie asks, picking up the gown.

I guess I shouldn't be surprised Allie's so comfortable here. Apparently, she used to work here, and she's a nurse. I always thought I was good in awkward situations, but I guess I was wrong because I've been nauseated since I walked into this place.

Heather chuckles. "That's what you get with a Greene. Those two have no idea how to mind their business when it comes to their grandchildren." She looks at Allie. "I actually think Dori's a bit more persistent, so be thankful he's not a Bailey."

Allie's gaze falls to mine. "They must've had a dry spell when I worked here."

"The only good thing is that they bribe us with awesome food." Heather winks and Allie laughs.

"Thanks, Heather," she says.

"No problem. Congratulations, you two." She smiles and walks out the door, shutting it behind her.

"Mind watching the door? I don't want my ass shown to everyone who walks by since your grandma can't seem to stop herself."

"I'll go outside." I walk to the door.

"Why? You've seen me naked. Just the other day actually." She raises an eyebrow in my direction.

That reminder brings up a mental image and all my blood rushes to my dick as I study the mental image to which she's referring. Her rounded belly—I now understand why it's bigger than one would anticipate. But she's gorgeous nonetheless. I've never found pregnant women attractive, but there's something about Allie carrying *my* babies that does it for me.

"I'll turn my back to you." I face the door, and there's a poster showing the size of the baby from conception to full term.

I study the diagram, wondering if twins change the scale of how big they are right now, while I try to ignore the sound of her undressing behind me. I do everything in my power not to peek over my shoulder. That would be inappropriate.

Then instead of zippers and buttons, I hear grunting and sighing.

"Great." She sighs.

"What's wrong?" I ask.

"Nothing. I got some of the ultrasound gel on my shirt under my sweater. I'm going to take it off, so it doesn't get on my pants. I can just wear my sweater." There's more grunting and groaning until she says my name as if razor blades are lining her throat.

"Yeah?" I say, keeping my feet planted where they are.

"I'm sorry, but—"

"Allie, it's okay. I know this is all a lot and we're both

unsure how to proceed. I guess we have to find our way back to friendship. I—"

"No," she says, and I stop talking. "My shirt is stuck in my hair. Can you help me?"

I unsuccessfully try to stop my lips from tipping into a devilish grin and start to turn around.

"Close your eyes!" she yelps.

I stop where I am. "I can't close my eyes and fix this for you."

"I'll guide you." There's desperation in her tone.

"I've already fallen on the floor today. If I bang my shin too, I'm gonna be pissed." I close my eyes and turn around. "Direct me over to you."

"Thank you. Okay, walk forward."

I take a couple of steps as if I'm on some weird new reality show where they're going to make me do stupid shit for a woman. I keep my hands by my side because there's no way I'm doing the Frankenstein walk.

"A little to your left," she says.

I step to the side and my right leg bangs into something hard. "Allie..."

"Sorry, sorry. I thought I could do it. A little more to your left."

"No shit."

Giving up all hope that she'll guide me where I need to go, I extend my hands in front of me, feeling the exam table, the paper crinkling under my palm.

"Two more steps."

My shoe sticks to the linoleum, causing me to lose my footing, and I reach forward to grab anything to stop me before I fall headfirst. My hands land on soft flesh, and I pop my eyes open to find myself holding Allie's bra-covered tits.

"Fisher!"

"Shit. I'm sorry."

She stares down at where my hands are still attached. "You can stop touching them now."

Damn, they're bigger and fleshier than before and my dick erects to half-mast to show his praise. I let my hands drop. "Can we work out some deal that lets me motorboat them?"

She slaps my arm with her free hand, and I chuckle. She's holding her shirt out from her hair that looks like a bird's nest. "Help me, please."

"Okay, okay. Hold tight."

I go around to the back of her to see what's going on. Her hair is wrapped around one of the buttons on her shirt.

"Now you've seen me naked *and* felt me up." There's displeasure in her voice, so I try to make a joke of what just happened.

"I'm a little offended you didn't get turned on with my hands on your tits."

"Why would I be turned on?"

"Aren't they sensitive?" I really wish I could stop being so inquisitive about her sex drive. Maybe it's because I know that I won't get to sleep with anyone until after these babies are born and we've settled into whatever family arrangement we decide on. Even then, if she's living with me, having sex with someone else would feel like a shitty thing to do. I'm not exactly looking forward to being celibate for the better part of a year.

"A little. They're heavy."

I suck in my groan while I try to unwrap her hair and she laughs.

"Sorry," she says.

"Stop apologizing. That said, if you ever need me to take the edge off one night, I'm your guy."

"We can't cross that line again, Fisher." Her tone is serious, but at the same time, she steps back closer to me. Her ass in danger of having my hard dick pressed into it.

I swallow. "Actually, maybe we need to talk about that."

If she doesn't use me to get off, will she go to someone else? Anger slices through me when I imagine her riding some guy with her swollen belly extended in front of her, her tits in his hands and my babies inside her. Just the thought feels like a punch to the gut.

"How is the shirt thing going?" She raises her hands to her hair to check for herself.

"Almost done. Relax." I get one button free, but I see that there's another one to contend with. "Are you planning on dating?"

"Do you honestly think I'd find someone who wants to have sex with a woman carrying twins?" She blows out a breath. "I've already reconciled myself to the fact that it's dildos and vibrators until after I finish breastfeeding. It'll be a sad, sad day when I can't reach between my legs anymore."

My dick hardens further, and I inch back, not wanting to offend her. "Good, because I don't want some guy's johnson that close to my babies."

I free the shirt and she must feel the relief on her scalp because she turns around to face me—surely to give me her dramatic expression of annoyance—but my gaze falls to her tits in her lace bra that she's trying to cover with one arm across them.

"What? You know I'm protective." I place my hand on her stomach and she tracks my movement with her eyes.

"I know, but really, you don't have to worry about it."

I put my other hand on her stomach, stepping closer because of how turned on I am. "Maybe we can come to an arrangement since we're both stuck being celibate for a while. Maybe we should take advantage of this no-condom-necessary situation we've found ourselves in." I inch closer, totally thinking with my dick.

Allie loves nipple play and I'm sure I could get her as turned on as me if she let me near them again.

"That's asking for trouble. We both know that." Her voice is husky and lacking conviction, so I opt to tell her exactly what's on my mind.

I take my hands off her and lock eyes with her. "Allie, I really wanna fuck you."

She tilts her head up, her gorgeous eyes staring at mine. She's wavering. I see it in the way her shoulders have fallen and how her mouth is slightly parted. "Do you have to tell me everything on your mind?"

If she only knew half the shit I was holding in. "Yes, when it can only benefit us."

There's a knock on the door and I pull her toward me, covering her with my body.

"Not yet," Allie says, but Stella must not have heard because she opens the door anyway.

Instead of looking at us, she's turned and talking to Ethel and Dori about patient privacy—which means it's my grandmother and her friend who see Allie in only her panties, pressed up against me. Dori nudges Ethel's arm and they smile.

"Oh, we forgot Midge is in the car," Dori says and the two walk down the hall.

Stella shakes her head and looks up. "So sorry, I'll be back in a couple minutes."

She slams the door, but the damage is done. My grandma and her delusional friend think Allie and I are on our way to being a couple. Two of the worst people to find me in this compromising situation.

AFTER THE EXAM WITH ALLIE, I stop at Jed's to help move a couch, then I go home to shower and get ready for my dinner with Allie.

I hear noise downstairs when I step out of the shower.

"Who the hell's here?" I yell from the top of the stairs, about a second from grabbing my gun.

"There's no reason to swear," my dad's voice booms from below.

I wrap a towel around myself and head down the stairs to find my dad putting groceries in the fridge. "Funny thing, I'm old enough to buy my own groceries now, Dad."

He doesn't even grant me a glance, placing a carton of eggs in the fridge. "Then do it. Especially now."

The fridge door shuts, and I wait for the real reason he's here.

He sighs in what sounds like resignation. "You're gonna have to grow up now."

There it is. The whole reason I haven't sought out my dad—I don't want the lecture. I remember Jed telling me the same thing and realize how he must've felt when he first found out he had a toddler. At least I'm being granted some time to get used to the idea of being a father.

"Thanks for coming, but I'm meeting Allie for dinner." I glance at the clock above the stove to see that I have another hour. There isn't a rush, but he doesn't need to know that.

"Sit down, Fisher." Dad eyes the table and chairs.

I've sat at this table my entire life. A lot of memories live here, from my mom telling me I couldn't throw ice balls at my brothers to my dad scolding Cam and me for a party we threw when we were freshmen. Most of the memories are good, but damn, the lectures given here. This table can probably recite some of my parents' wisdom itself.

But I won't disobey my dad, so I sit down. "Can I at least get dressed?"

"No." He sits at the table. "Your grandmother called me."

I lower my head until my forehead thumps on the table.

"Chin up, son," my dad says.

"What did she tell you?"

"That Allie is having twins?" His eyes are wide and disbelieving.

I sit up and growl at the fact Grandma can't keep this to herself. And also, how the hell did she find out?

"She also said that you and Allie were having sex at the doctor's office."

"What?"

My dad holds up his hand and suddenly I'm fifteen again. "I don't need to hear your excuses. You're a grown adult, but do you really think sleeping with her is going to solve your problem? You two cannot be in a relationship unless you're both committed, otherwise it's sure to end in disaster—for you, Allie, and your babies. Last I checked, you were on the single train."

"I am, and we weren't having sex. Her shirt got stuck in her hair..." I groan. It doesn't matter what I say at this point. "Can't she keep anything to herself?"

"No, she can't. And normally I wouldn't bother coming over here, but you need to remember that you're the sheriff and this town is small. The last thing you need is to piss people off. You'll need your job to take care of your family."

"Do you think I don't know that? Fuck, Dad, I'm not Jed." I feel a little like an asshole for making the comparison to my stepbrother, but he did not handle the news that he was a father well. I'm insulted that my dad would even question whether or not I would step up.

"Language," he says.

I look over his shoulder out the back window. "I offered for her to move in with me. She doesn't want to."

"You two are both grown. She doesn't need to move in."

"She lives in Lake Starlight," I snap. Why am I the only one who thinks she needs to be closer, under my roof preferably?

Dad grabs a bag of chips that's sitting in the center of the table and opens it. "Then work it out with her, but if her living here is going to cause the two of you to fall into bed, I'd suggest she move in here and you stay above the garage."

"It doesn't matter what I offer, she's not gonna want to do what I want and live here." I sound like a spoiled thirteen-year-old kid and my dad's facial expression says as much.

"Listen, I know you'll do right by these babies. It's just who you are. But it's time to deal with your shit, Fish. I've sat back and let you carry around this chip on your shoulder, be the grumpy guy. If you want to do the best job you can for those kids, you need to sort yourself out. Figure out what's holding you back from wanting a real relationship with a woman."

"You're right. I will raise my kids to the best of my ability, but I sure as shit am not gonna marry Allie just because she's having my kids." I don't bother telling my dad, but Allie would say no anyway. She's hell-bent on Prince Charming riding in on a white horse, and I'm pretty sure if I was the man of anyone's dreams, I'd be riding in on a black horse.

"I'm not saying that, but what I am saying is that you've avoided dealing with whatever it is that won't let you love a woman for long enough. You wanna love those kids to the best of your ability you need to sort yourself out, that's all. Oh, and you should lock your dick up until the two of you figure out what you want, no matter how hungry you are for her."

"Believe me, I'm starving," I grumble low enough that I don't think he hears.

"I'll let you get ready now." He slides away from the table. "Oh, and Marla wanted me to tell you that Allie's welcome to stay at our house."

"Of course."

Marla opens her house to everyone. I don't much care what my dad thinks though—Allie and the babies are moving in here with me. At least on a temporary basis.

"See you later, son. And listen, I told your grandma to let you and Allie put the news out there that you're having twins. Your secret is safe with me." He walks out my back door, and I wait to hear his truck pull out of the driveway.

Maybe he's got a point. Just remembering my hands on her tits earlier has my towel lifting between my legs. Fuck, I gotta get this arousal out of my system before I meet her for dinner. I head upstairs and turn the shower back on.

By the time I finish my second shower, Allie's name is slipping from my lips.

Allie

Truth or Dare Brewery is busy for a weeknight, and as soon as I walk in, I realize I should've suggested more neutral territory, especially after Nikki's gossip segment on the local radio station.

"Baby?" Emilia, Jed's daughter, comes over to me, her hand outstretched to my stomach.

"Em!" I look away from Emilia to find Molly weaving frantically through the tables, desperation in her eyes. "I'm so sorry." She pulls the little girl's hand off my stomach. "Emilia, you can't do that."

Emilia's lower lip trembles and tears fill her eyes. Molly picks her up and comforts her.

"It's really okay," I say. "She's really grown so much since the barbecue." I'm going to pretend that I didn't see her last week with Molly and Jed in the hospital room when Fisher found out I was pregnant. Hopefully Molly will play along.

"Right? She's fascinated with babies, and she probably remembers..." She lets her words die off. "We ran into a babysitting issue, so she's here with us for a bit." She glances over her shoulder toward Jed, who's serving customers behind the bar. "Anyway, I'm super sorry." She steps back, then steps forward again, rubbing Emilia's back and smiling. "Congratulations."

Awareness dawns on me that Emilia and my babies will be related. Jed and Fisher are stepbrothers, and whether or not I'm with Fisher, a relationship between my unborn babies and Emilia will likely exist.

"Does she understand that the baby is Fisher's and will be her cousin?" I leave the plural out of my sentence, not sure if Fisher wants his family to know he's having twins yet.

Molly's lips tip up. She's really beautiful, with her long dark hair and pink pouty lips. If I'm honest, I've always been jealous of girls like her. The ones who appear so confident and sure of themselves. "She doesn't fully understand, but she knows that Fisher is her uncle."

"Uncle!" Emilia shouts with an outstretched hand toward the door and a big smile.

Sure enough, Fisher walks into Truth or Dare in a pair of worn jeans and a jacket which he promptly removes. Underneath, he's wearing a faded T-shirt that shows his tattoos sneaking out from under the fabric in all directions. I've seen them all, but I never had the time to trace them and question their meaning.

Emilia squirms enough that Molly lowers her to the floor, and she runs through the maze of tables and chairs like a professional downhill skier, screaming "Uncle!"

Fisher takes no time to swoop Emilia into his arms, throwing her in the air before catching her. I glance around the room. It's as though all conversations have stopped so people can gawk at the spectacle. I can't believe he's the father of my babies.

"What's up? Working your shift?" he asks his little niece. Fisher stops at a few tables to say hello to the patrons who force themselves on him.

Emilia turns toward me. "Baby!"

Fisher's dark eyes pierce mine, and either the twins are getting active early or he's causing butterflies in my tummy.

"Want to know a secret?" Fisher lowers Emilia so she stands on a chair, then cups his hand around his mouth to whisper in her ear.

Emilia's eyes widen and she whips around, staring at my belly again. "Two?"

Molly shoots me a hesitant smile laced with worry. I'm already the town news, so who cares if a four-year-old knows we're having twins?

"Hey, Mol, I'm only one man over here," Jed yells from behind the bar.

"Come on, Emilia, you need to go back and color until your babysitter shows up." Molly glances at the clock. "I have no idea what's taking her so long."

"She can hang with us," I say. If we're busy keeping Emilia busy, I won't have to face the conversation ahead.

Fisher's eyebrows shoot up. "No, she can't. Sorry, Mol, but—"

"No. I get it." She holds out her hand. "Come on, Emilia."

Emilia's shoulders slump and she lowers her head, walking away.

"Way to kill a little girl's night," I say before sipping the water the waitress brought over earlier.

"I'm her favorite uncle. She'll get over it." Fisher shrugs and sets his coat on the back of his chair. And just like that, his grumpy side reappears. He flags down the waitress who wastes no time in rushing over.

"What's up, Fish?" I ignore the pang of annoyance in my chest from her using a nickname.

"Can I have a beer and the quesadillas?" He looks at me. "What would you like?"

"I'll have the fish tacos," I say.

The waitress smiles at Fisher, not me, and turns back to the kitchen area.

"Friend of yours?" I ask.

"I grew up here and I'm the sheriff. Not really anyone I don't know."

Fair enough.

A devilish smile crosses Fisher's lips. "I like you jealous."

"I'm not jealous." I distract myself with another sip of water. As if I already don't have to pee so much these days that it's like my bladder is a water tower.

"Don't worry, you're the one having my babies."

I spit out my water and it sprays all over the table. He doesn't react except to grab a few napkins the waitress left with my water and clean up.

"Aren't you full of yourself?"

"I have twenty-twenty vision." He shrugs. I stare blankly at him, and he chuckles. "What?"

"Nothing. Let's just get this going." I dig into my bag and pull out a small notepad and pen.

His eyebrows raise. "What's that?"

"So I can take notes." My memory is like a colander these days.

"Notes?"

"Here you go, Fish." The waitress slides a beer across the table.

"Thanks, Ivy." He sips the beer, chuckling to himself.

"What's so funny?"

"The fact that you think we need notes to figure this out."

I drop the pen and cross my arms.

He lowers his beer to the coaster and licks his lips, which sends a zing of excitement between my thighs. That night we were together was hard and fast with no foreplay, but I guarantee Fisher knows how to use that tongue.

"Seems pretty easy to me," he says. "You're having my babies. You work in Sunrise Bay, but you live in Lake Starlight—alone. You move in with me and we figure out what to do long term after the babies arrive, but I'll be completely honest, I don't see why we can't just cohabitate there together."

I huff. "That seems a little premature. I'm not moving in with you."

"I'm not asking for us to move into the same room, but I'm not cool with being a weekend dad, you know. My schedule isn't all that flexible, so having the kids at my house works better for me."

I do a double blink and stare at him. "Better for you?"

He swallows another sip of his beer and nods. God, I want to throat punch him.

"I'm the one whose body is being pushed to the limit here. Shouldn't we do what works better for me?"

"It *is* better for you." There isn't an ounce of humor in his expression.

"How do you figure?"

"You'd be closer to work. If something should happen, I'm a sheriff who also knows enough medical stuff to get us by in the event that I have to deliver the babies."

"You're not delivering the babies!" I say, horrified and so loud that a few tables stop eating to get a look at us.

"I'm saying if need be. Not like it's actually going to happen." He sips his beer again.

"I think you need to get this whole me moving in with you thing out of your head."

Lucky for me, the food is delivered by our lovely waitress, Ivy, and I unwrap my silverware to eat. I'm starving. I know I haven't been eating enough lately. The stress of this whole situation makes it worse.

"I swear I'm a good roommate," he says. "I clean, I cook, I'll learn to put the toilet seat down."

I eye him while taking a huge bite of my fish taco.

"What? I've only had guy roommates before. You can't blame me."

"Not that. Come on, Fisher. We had a one-night stand. It's not like we're best friends or were ever in a relationship." I finish my first taco, my stomach finally satisfied.

"We're friends."

I laugh and down my taco with a sip of my water. "Friends call friends back."

He pushes his hand through his hair and my fingertips tingle with the memory of how thick and silky his hair felt between my fingers. "I'm not good with awkward situations."

I'll never tell Fisher how much it hurt when he didn't answer or call me back. It was a punch to the gut that left me winded. I knew in the month of silence after we slept with each other that my feelings that had started to grow for him weren't reciprocated. But because of the reason for my call, it stung more that he couldn't even bother to call me back. Then again, you can't change a zebra's stripes and Fisher's will never change. It's best I figured that out early on.

"And you want me to live with you? You don't think that will be awkward?"

"As I see it, I'll just have to get over it."

I wipe my mouth and sigh, placing my hands in my lap. "How do you see this playing out? We make a schedule of who does the shopping and who does the cooking?"

He shrugs. "Figure we'll see how it goes."

"And if you meet a girl, should I have to endure listening

to you fucking her in the room next door?" There's probably more fire in my voice than should be, but I can't help myself.

"I told you, I'm not going to be hooking up with anyone anytime soon."

I pick up my second fish taco but lower it for a moment. "If you're talking about the twins and me living there, what are you going to do, stop fucking altogether?"

He cringes.

Finally, I have him thinking rationally. He should stop this whole nonsense about us living together now if he can't keep his dick in his pants.

"Like I said, one step at a time."

I place down the uneaten taco. I've had almost five months to think these things through and he's only had a week, so I need to spell it out for him. "Fisher, we're going to be in each other's lives for at least the next eighteen years. Really, we're stuck together until one of us dies. We cannot afford to start this on a bad note. I think I should just stay at my apartment for now, and maybe I'll look for something closer to Sunrise Bay after the babies are born."

He shakes his head like a temperamental two-year-old. "Nope. We'll make it work, Allie."

I blow out a frustrated breath.

The doors of the brewery open and in strolls Ethel and Dori.

"I swear they installed a tracking device on me," I mumble, making Fisher turn around.

"You befriended them," he says, tearing apart his quesadilla.

"I wanted to learn the matchmaking ropes, not be stalked by them. They're working on something, believe me."

Ethel waves and Dori takes the reins and forges over to us. "What a surprise."

"Is it really?" I lean back and cross my arms.

"I hoped I'd run into you. I tried to call, but you didn't answer."

I glance at my phone that's face down on the table. I haven't heard it ping or ring. "Really?" I pick it up, ready to prove her wrong, but I see that it says missed call from Dori Bailey. Apparently I've had it on silent since the doctor's office visit. Damn it. "Sorry."

Dori gives me a smug, satisfied smile. "I wanted to tell you you can't go home tonight. The bathroom in the unit above yours leaked down into your apartment and there's a lot of damage."

Fisher chuckles, but when I cut him a glare, he tries to stop himself—unsuccessfully.

"Don't try to push us together." I pick up my phone to call my upstairs neighbor, Bert, to see if this story is fictional.

Both the elderly ladies hold up their hands.

Jed walks Emilia over with her backpack on. "Here she is. I'll pick her up tomorrow morning. Thanks, Bibi, we owe you."

Bert doesn't answer and I groan. They're probably making up the whole thing.

"You're having Grandma take Emilia for the night? They're driving her back there?" Fisher asks.

"Lake Starlight isn't an hour away. It's twenty minutes at most," I say, since he acts as if the neighboring town is at the top of a mountain.

"We're desperate," Jed says.

"Must be." Fisher shakes his head.

Ethel takes Emilia's hand and smacks the back of Fisher's head. "I'm her great-grandmother and fully capable of having Emilia stay at my place for the night. They're setting up a Candyland game right now at Northern Lights."

"Oh, Candyland," Fisher says like a teenage boy making fun of his parents.

"The arthritis in this hand isn't that bad, I'll smack you again."

While Fisher argues with his grandma, Dori slides out the chair next to me. "I have a contractor on it, and we'll get you back in as soon as possible." She pats my hand.

"And what am I supposed to do now?"

"I'm sure you'll figure something out. I don't want you going in there with the water. What if you slip? Liability."

I groan. "Fine. I'll see if I can get into Glacier Pointe."

Dori smiles. "Make sure you tell them you know me and give them your name. My granddaughter's husband owns the place, and he can probably figure something out."

I look at her skeptically and dial up the resort in Lake Starlight. It only takes the receptionist a minute after getting my information to tell me there's some big ski event going on and they're fully booked. I could go to Stella's, but that would mean sleeping on the couch. I'm not sure my back can handle it.

"I'll try Sunbay Inn."

"I just saw Mandi and she's all full. Winter activities, you know?" Ethel chimes in.

Fisher opens up his arms. "Mi casa es su casa."

I sigh, succumbing to my fate for at least one night. But tomorrow, I'm finding another place to stay. There's no way I can sleep under the same roof as Fisher Greene without wanting to sleep with him again.

Fisher

Allie doesn't believe Dori and is convinced she and my grandma plotted to get Allie to stay at my house, so we're in my truck, driving to her apartment in Lake Starlight to see if there is in fact water damage.

"Don't you know how much they meddle in people's lives?" Allie's foot taps along the floorboard. "Always pushing people together. To think I wanted in on that at one point." She shakes her head while she absentmindedly rubs her swollen belly.

For whatever reason, I have to fight the urge to reach over and do the same.

"You were upset that they didn't ask you to take part in my family's barbecue this summer," I remind her. Both women had shown up with an agenda.

She huffs. "And you were really upset that they wanted to set me up with either your best friend or your step-brother."

"I was not." That's a complete lie. I saw red when they thought Allie should be with Cam. He's a player and will always be a player.

She runs her hands over her belly and glares at me. "I'm pretty sure that's the reason these little ones are snug in my stomach."

I guffaw. "I wasn't the only horny one."

"Lonely. I was lonely."

I clench my hand over my heart, keeping one hand on the steering wheel. "That's a slice to the heart."

"Um... you only slept with me to prove something. What? I still haven't figured out."

She's so right all the time, it annoys the crap out of me. I slept with her—in part, because yeah, I was horny—to make sure she was off-limits to my family and friends. But I still can't figure out why. Sure, I liked her, and it did piss me off that Grandma and her blue-haired friend didn't even consider me as a candidate to fix her up with. But it makes no sense, because my dad was right this afternoon when he said I'm on the single train without any plans of stepping off. Still, Allie's comment smarts and I go on defense.

"Is your reason much better? That could be any schmuck's baby in your belly." I eye her stomach.

She swivels in my direction. "What are you implying?"

"You said you were lonely."

"Yes, but I don't just put a 'for rent' sign around my neck and wait for any ol' fool to show up every time I'm lonely."

I laugh. She huffs and sits straight with her arms crossed.

"I didn't mean it like that. I just meant I slept with you because it was you, and you make it sound like you slept with me because I had a dick."

"Is that hurt I hear in your tone?" She doesn't sound as angry as she was a moment ago.

"Hell yeah. I'm not arrogant, but I don't think I'm that bad to look at." I rub one hand over my scruff.

She shakes her head and sighs. "Jeez, Fisher. I slept with you because I was starting to like you as more than a friend, *plus* I was lonely. Does that make it better?"

"It heals the ego slightly." One corner of my mouth tilts up.

"Good."

I pull up outside her apartment and it's like she can't escape the truck fast enough. A bald man is walking up the outside set of stairs to the apartment and she calls to him. "Ernie!"

The man turns around as I climb out of my truck to join her. He watches me while Allie calls out again.

"Is my apartment really flooded?" she asks, climbing the stairs.

Ernie finally looks at her. "Bert flushed the toilet and something broke off, but he was late for work and didn't know. It wasn't until the water went through your apartment and down to Nancy's that anyone found it."

I follow Allie up the painted outside stairway. Does she really think she should walk up these stairs every day? She's only going to be getting bigger, and at some point, I assume she won't be able to see her feet.

A big sign on her door says, "Do not enter," but Allie inserts her key anyway.

"How long are you out of your place for?" She turns to Ernie, who's now walking down the stairs toward us. He's short and wearing a striped sweater and khakis.

I use the distraction to open the door and step in before her.

"I don't know. Dori said she has people coming by tomorrow. Bert's suffering from some high anxiety right now. Afraid of Dori, you know?"

Bert and Ernie. Does Big Bird live here too?

I stand inside the door and Allie stands outside while Ernie keeps glancing at me.

I stretch out my hand. "Fisher."

He shakes my hand limply and mumbles, "Ernie."

"Oh yeah, sorry." Allie waves her finger back and forth between us.

"But it was weird, Dori wasn't all that upset," Ernie says. "She said mistakes happen."

I don't know Dori really well, but she's my grandma's best friend and seems like a ballbuster, so her reaction is somewhat surprising.

Allie shoots me a look. I'm starting to see why she might think they're trying to force us together, which isn't all that crazy now that she's carrying my babies.

"Anyway, I better get back to Bert. Just wanted to grab a few things." He lifts his suitcase at his feet.

"Where are you staying?" Allie asks eagerly.

I roll my eyes. Why can't she just accept that she's staying with me?

"Dori got us set up at Glacier Pointe. Her son-in-law gave us a great deal. Honestly, like I said, she's been more than great about this whole situation."

"How nice for you," she mumbles.

They say their goodbyes and agree to call one another with updates.

Allie growls, entering the apartment. "I swear those two."

Everything looks fine when we first walk in. Her apartment is exactly what I would've imagined—a mix of colors that somehow all fit, knickknacks that serve no purpose on her furniture, and her couch looks comfortable. The remote is sitting on the coffee table instead of being thrown on the couch like it usually is at my place. Although everything has its place, it's still warm and homey.

"This is a nice place," I say.

"Yeah, I moved to Lake Starlight after spending time

with Stella and Kingston here. I really loved the small-town feel. But now that I'm the subject of the gossip mill, I don't have as much adoration for small-town life." She cringes.

"I can talk to Nikki." I will if it bothers Allie that much. For me, I fluff it off, but I've been in Sunrise Bay my entire life, so I'm used to the gossip.

"No, it's fine. I'm the one who let the sheriff knock me up."

"I think we can figure out a way to word that better."

She laughs and walks down the hallway. Her screech rings out moments later.

I rush to follow, and sure enough, the hallway ceiling has a bunch of water damage that extends down the wall to the floor.

"You go wait on the couch." I place my hands on Allie's shoulders and pull her back.

"I'm fine. I'm just going to the bedroom. Might as well grab some stuff while I'm here."

"Be careful. We aren't even supposed to be in here." I follow her into the bedroom and find the vibe to be the same as the rest of her place, except for the unmade bed.

She pulls the sheets up and tucks them under. "I was busy, okay?"

"Do you think I care if you make your bed?"

"I care. Now I just need to pack a suitcase and we can get out of here."

She reaches into her closet, but I reach in front of her and take the bag from her hands. "You do know you're pregnant?"

"And you do know that pregnant women can do things, right? Are you gonna start following me around on my shifts?"

"Maybe," I say, dead serious. If I had my way, Allie would

spend her pregnancy at home. I have to think that carrying twins, that's a distinct possibility the further she gets into her pregnancy.

She blows out another annoyed breath. Those breathy sounds of hers are starting to turn me on.

I place the suitcase on the bed, and she opens some drawers in the dresser, pulls out clothes, and puts them in the suitcase. "We need to lay down rules if this is gonna work."

I set my hands on my hips. "I'm not a fan of rules."

"You're the sheriff," she deadpans.

I shrug. "Let me clarify—I don't like being told what to do."

"You sure like giving the orders."

I could be reading her wrong, but it feels as though innuendo laces her words. I have to wonder if she's thinking of the night we were together.

"Like you said, I'm the sheriff." I sit on the edge of the bed and watch her try to conceal her panties and bras as she shoves them in the zippered compartment of the suitcase.

"Well, if I'm going to stay with you, you need to let me live my life. I may be pregnant, but I'm fully capable of doing things for myself."

"Okay." I hold up my hands. "I'll try."

"And there's no walking around half naked."

"That's a buzzkill. You mean—"

She interrupts. "You have a shirt on at all times."

I bite my lip to stop my smile. The only reason she would want that rule in place is because she's attracted to me. "Okay, but just know that you don't have to abide by that rule. Walk around naked if you'd like."

She glares at me, and it seems that's a turn-on too. Damn it all to hell.

"Let's just get me packed and get out of here. Hopefully Dori can work her magic and I'll be out of your hair in a few days."

By the look of the hallway and the bathroom, I would lean toward a few weeks at a minimum.

"If we're making up rules, I have one of my own."

She pauses putting clothes into her suitcase. "What?"

"Stop fighting me about living with me. Until this apartment is ready, you stay with me without acting like it's an inconvenience. After the apartment is ready, we can see how things are going and decide what'll happen from there."

She turns to grab more clothes, not answering me right away. "Fine," she says in a low voice I barely catch. "I'll try."

"Then I'll try to keep a shirt on."

She whips around and I laugh.

"Come on, we need to get out of here before we fall through the floorboards." I zip up her suitcase and pick it up off the bed.

"Hold on." She snags a picture off her dresser and holds it to her chest. "Ready."

"Who's that?" I eye her hands clutching the frame. It's clearly important to her.

"My grandparents."

"Did they raise you or something?"

She follows me out of her apartment, snagging some other items on our way out. "No, I have parents. But after I graduated, my parents decided that they wanted warmer weather, so they moved to Hawaii. My grandparents are kind of like role models." Pink colors her cheeks and damn if it doesn't endear her to me more.

"Why are they your role models?"

We walk out to my truck, and I shove her suitcase in the back.

She opens the other back door and shoves her extra things onto the floorboard. Everything except the picture, which she takes up to the passenger seat with her. "No reason."

I can tell she's lying.

"Come on. You can trust me. Might as well learn things about one another." I shrug as though I can take it or leave it, but truth is, I want to know what she's hiding.

She seems to think it over for a minute, then turns the picture toward me as I'm backing up.

Before I put the truck in drive, I glance over. "They look like a nice couple."

"They were in love. Deeply and passionately in love. My grandfather wasn't the same after she died. He passed away only a few months after her. I think he couldn't bear to be without her." She stares at the picture with a sad smile, running her fingers over the glass.

"And that's where the fairy tale was born, huh?"

She smiles at me and nods. It's a simple reason that I should've predicted.

Allie isn't a princess type of girl. She's not looking for a prince to take care of her. The little girl inside her just wants to be loved wholly. Too bad she picked the wrong guy to have a one-night stand with, because I'm not capable of loving anyone the way she deserves to be loved.

Chapter Ten

Allie

It's been three days since I agreed to stay at Fisher's place. Though for the record, I didn't have much of a choice. Dori made sure of that. Since I've witnessed her and Ethel's scheming before, I wouldn't put it past them to inconvenience Bert, Ernie, and Nancy just to get what they want—Fisher and I together.

I'm not sure what it will take for them to understand that Fisher doesn't want a wife and I don't want a husband who doesn't want commitment. Call me crazy, but that's kind of a deal breaker.

Things have been going well, I suppose. He works a lot. More than I thought, but he's been busy dealing with the Netflix bandit and was over at Sam Klein's last night. Whoever is responsible had the guts to break into the mayor's house.

As a thank you for letting me stay here, I've decided to clean Fisher's entire house and cook him dinner. Once the chili is in the Crock-Pot and the cornbread is cooling, I straighten up the family room—vacuuming and dusting and putting away all the game controllers. The one night he was home, he sat in front of the television the entire time while I went upstairs to read a book about what to expect when you're pregnant.

Had I known this was what living together would be like, I wouldn't have fought so hard against it. The commute to work is nice. Except for driving home at three in the morning and carrying bear spray up to the door in case a bear pops out of the woods.

Headlights shine through the windows of my… er… Fisher's living room. I peek through the curtains to see his truck come to a stop. He climbs out and I watch him walk the opposite way then stop, staring out through a sea of trees on the other side of the property. He slides his hands into the pockets of his slacks and stands for a moment, not going any farther. He doesn't pull out his flashlight or inch forward, just stares ahead. What is he thinking about?

It must be five minutes before he turns and shakes his head, walking toward the house. I rush back into the kitchen, not wanting him to see that I was spying on him.

"Honey, I'm home," he says, his usual joke when he comes home every night, and makes his way into the kitchen. "Oh, a candlelit dinner? Does this mean we're changing up the rules?"

I roll my eyes, regretting that I lit the new candle I bought today, and turn around in my sweatpants and a sweatshirt I borrowed from him—which will probably make it clear that romance is not on my mind. I badly need to buy some maternity clothes.

"Shirt rule is still in effect," I say.

"Seems unfair that you can wear my clothes, but I can't wear yours."

"What do you want to borrow?" I lift the lid off the Crock-Pot and stir the chili. More for something to do than out of necessity. Fisher still pulls this uncomfortable feeling out of me. I have no idea how to behave around a man I'd started to fall for, slept with, ended up pregnant by, then didn't speak to for months, only to find out he wants to be Mister Mom now that he knows he's going to be a father.

"Your panties."

I swear I'm going to give myself a neck injury from the number of times I shake my head at what comes out of his mouth. Before I got to know Fisher, I thought he was this sullen, grumpy guy, but he's got a dry sense of humor that makes me laugh. Especially when he delivers the joke with no humor on his part.

"They aren't all that sexy right now. Nothing about me is sexy right now."

I put the lid back on the chili and cut the cornbread to put in a basket, but he comes up behind me. His hands slide around my waist to my stomach, and he rests his chin on my shoulder. I can't deny the euphoric sensation of having him so close that I can smell him. It's not cologne, just the fresh scent of soap and man.

"What are you doing?" I ask, frozen in place.

His hands run over my belly. "You're sexy as hell. I'd show you just how sexy you are, but you've sworn me off."

I open my mouth.

"I know. I know. We can't cross that line, but do not undermine how sexy you are carrying my babies. And for making dinner, I'll reward you with a foot rub tonight."

Just then one of the babies kicks where his left hand is and I feel his body tense behind mine. "Was that?" His voice is full of awe.

I nod, tears pricking my eyes. "Guess someone wanted to say hi."

The baby kicks again as though he or she understood me and Fisher rubs the area. "Amazing. That's our child."

He stays there for a moment and then backs away and I immediately miss the security of his arms.

Fisher goes up to take a shower while I finish dinner. The sound of running water spurs visuals of his naked body under a stream of water while soapy bubbles ripple down his abs and strong thighs.

I press my thighs together and shake my head. I can't go there. Fisher doesn't want a life partner. Just because he says sweet things and is attentive as hell doesn't mean that's changed. He's just a stand-up guy. A guy I shouldn't have waited so long to tell he was going to be a father. Regardless, becoming involved sexually with the father of my babies is a bad idea all around.

He barrels down the stairs like a teenage boy and emerges in the kitchen. He's wearing sweatpants, a worn T-shirt, and he's barefoot. Basically, he's like catnip to me. Although I have the same reaction when he's wearing his sheriff's uniform.

"Smells great," he says, heading to the fridge. "What do you want to drink?"

"I'll have water."

"Then I will too."

He sits down at the table, putting a bottle of water down for me and another for himself. I've already pulled out the sour cream, cheese, and crackers to go with the chili, so there isn't much else to do. I fill two bowls with chili and bring them to the kitchen table.

"If you'd rather eat in the family room, I understand."

"Nah, I like this. I don't eat dinner here very often. This is nice."

I sit and smile, then dip my spoon into the chili. He prepares his chili bowl and gets everything set before taking a bite.

My ego rises a little when I hear a moan slip from his lips. "This is awesome. What kind of meat is in here?"

"It's pork shoulder. Shredded, rather than ground beef."

He shoves another heaping spoonful into his mouth. "It's good. I've never had it like this before."

"Thanks. It's a family recipe my grandmother passed on to my mother and now to me."

"My mom used to make chili every Sunday during football season. I would groan and complain about how we always had the same thing, but after she died, I really missed those days. The smell would fill the house, the television would be on with games all day, my brothers and I would wrestle or mess around, and my dad would scream at the refs." He chuckles. "Chevelle would just play with her dolls or be hanging off Mom."

I look at him with a sad smile. "Those are good memories."

He glances up. I know enough about Fisher's family to know that his mother died and his dad married Marla years later, who happened to be divorced from Fisher's estranged uncle. I can't imagine what it's like to lose a parent. I'd be lost.

"Yeah." He pauses, almost like he's not sure he wants to go on. "She died when I was ten."

"I'm sorry."

He chuckles lightly. "Everyone says that, but it's been so long now... sometimes I wonder if the memories are real or something I've imagined."

"That memory seemed pretty vivid."

He nods. "Yeah. I can picture her so clearly. Reprimanding us for being too rough, yelling at my dad for not telling us to stop. But sometimes she'd come in and sit on the couch next to Dad and fall asleep or just lay her head on his shoulder. He'd wrap his arm around her and pull her closer. While she was beside him, he never yelled at the refs."

I smile, honored he's trusting me by opening up about this.

We eat in silence for a minute until he sets down his spoon and looks at me. "I get what you mean about your grandpa and grandma. My parents always displayed their love around us, and maybe if she wouldn't have died in a frozen pond, I might've believed that there's someone out there for everyone just like you do. I guess I went the opposite way."

I drink my water, wanting to ask more specifically how she died but not wanting to push the subject.

"Have you ever lost someone?" he asks.

"My grandparents."

He nods. "They were older, right?"

I open my mouth, but he's quick to interrupt.

"I'm not trying to say it's not a big deal because they were, I just... I guess I learned from a young age that bad things happen to good people, and no one has any control over it."

I swallow a mouthful of chili, taken aback by his raw honesty. Why is he trusting me with all this?

"That's why I want you here. I have control issues. I know I do. But I want to protect you and the babies as much as I can. I'm sorry if that bothers you."

He looks up from his bowl and our eyes lock. Is Fisher Greene really opening up his chest and giving me a glimpse of his beating heart?

"I—"

"Sorry, it was a really bad day today," he says. "There was a car accident up on the deserted part of Route 53. Car hit a deer. The guy survived, but he broke some ribs and his face was pretty messed up. Blood everywhere. It just proves my point that bad things happen every day."

Being a nurse, I understand what he's saying, but I guess I've always thought more about how many people I help. Just another example of how opposite Fisher and I are on most things.

"But he did survive."

"You know how many don't?" He buries his face in his chili, looking away from me. "But I get what you're saying. It just got me thinking about you and the babies. I did some research on twins, and there are a lot more complications than with a single baby."

My heart feels as if it fills with helium and wants to float out of my chest.

He researched.

He cares.

I run my hands over my belly. "Right now, everything is good and that's all we can think about."

"I'm responsible for putting us in this position."

"You didn't make the condom defective. It's neither of our faults. We thought we were being responsible."

He shrugs as though he's not agreeing with me, but he'll let it go.

That night was such a flurry. Clothes were torn off, hands couldn't move fast enough. Cursing, begging, pleading would have been the soundtrack until he sank into me and all I saw were stars.

"I'm the man, it's my responsibility to check the condom after."

I choke on the chili and struggle to eventually swallow. "Please rephrase that before I get upset."

He places his spoon down and leans back in his chair,

tipping it to rest on the back legs as if he's a teenager. "What? It's the truth."

"No, it's not. I could have asked you to make sure it was okay. They're coming, so there's no point in having this argument, but if that is your mentality, Fisher, then this is never going to work." I stand and take my chili with me. "And please don't think me staying here means I make dinner every night, wash your clothes, and iron your uniform."

Anger hijacks all rational thinking and I busy myself at the sink, wanting to clean up the kitchen so I can go to bed.

Fisher laughs from his seat. "Saying I'm responsible for the condom wasn't me revealing I have the same beliefs as a 1950s man. I've been cooking meals, washing my clothes—including ironing my uniform—for years by myself and I plan to continue to do that for many more years. You have it all wrong."

"You like control, you said it yourself." I turn around from the sink, wiping my hands on the dish towel, and cross my arms.

"Control as in I like to know you're safe."

I want to scream and beg why it matters to him, but he's made it clear. The babies are his concern. "Well, I'm here, aren't I?"

"Forced."

I throw my hands in the air, just as a horn honks outside. Fisher stands, and I follow him to the front of the house to see who it is.

"Why is there a U-Haul here?" I ask him, accusation clear in my tone.

"How the hell should I know?" He opens the door, and we step outside.

Dori pokes her head through the open window of the

passenger side of the truck. "Yoo-hoo! We've got your stuff, Allie, but we're going to need help unloading."

A truck pulls up after, honking the horn until it stops, and Cameron Baker climbs out. "Never thought I'd see the day where my best buddy moves in with a girl. Even if he stole her right out from under me." He gives us both a cheeky grin, then opens the lock from the back of the U-Haul and rolls up the door.

Ethel climbs out of the driver's side of the U-Haul.

I'm so confused. "Dori? Ethel?"

"Damage is worse than we first thought. Everything has to be restructured. Sorry, dear, you're here for the foreseeable future."

I stare blankly ahead, not understanding where my life went wrong. But I guess I know the answer to that question, don't I? It's when I let lust take over and got myself knocked up by a Greene.

Chapter Eleven

Fisher

"**M**ind telling me what the fuck is going on?" Cam lowers his side of the couch into the detached garage of my house.

We're going to store all Allie's stuff here until... well... I have no clue until when. I'd like her and the babies to stay here, but maybe I'm being unrealistic to think we can live in the same house for the next eighteen years while we raise our kids together, without being *together*. She wants a prince and I'm not up for being celibate for the rest of my life, so we'll have to figure something out. Maybe we can build houses near one another or something.

"What do you want to know?" I ask.

He sits on the couch and crosses his legs so his ankle rests on his knee. "This is comfy. Is this where the babies were made?" He inspects it as though he's expecting to find evidence or something. It's worrisome that he doesn't seem like he'd be grossed out if he did. My best friend is unique in many ways.

"No, it's not."

"Were you at your house when you did the deed?"

I run my hand through my hair and sit on a chair from her kitchen.

According to Dori, everyone is out of the building for at

least a month and maybe longer because the structure is unsafe. I knew we shouldn't have been in there grabbing her things. Dori had Cam and two of her grandsons pack everyone's stuff. Supposedly Bert, Ernie, and Nancy all had U-Hauls filled too. I'm not sure I completely believe that the damage is as bad as she says, but I'm not gonna call the old lady a liar. My grandma might kick me in the nuts if I disrespected one of her friends.

"I'm going to be a dad and I can't stand the thought of something happening and me not being there. That about sums up what's going on. Oh, and my grandma and Dori are up to their usual meddling ways."

Cam raises his eyebrows. "And you think this is the best option?"

I shrug, still unsure about all my life decisions at this point. Instead of going off a strategic plan, I'm going with my gut and my feelings, which isn't me, and Cam damn well knows it.

"You're aware that she's a human being and you can't control her, right?"

"I'm not trying to control her. We have an arrangement."

He chuckles. "This should be good."

Cam waits for me to fill in the blanks, but I'm not really a "sharing is caring" kinda guy, especially when it comes to my struggles. While some of my siblings sought out therapy after my mom passed, I pretended I wasn't in pain, resorting to crying late at night when everyone was asleep. I acted as though I was fine and wasn't affected by my mom drowning only steps away from the house I still live in. Especially since Chevelle had it the worst. She blamed herself for what happened and I'm fairly sure she still does.

"I have to wear a shirt at all times, and she stays at my house without giving me trouble."

Cam smiles before he bends over in a fit of manic laughter. He holds his hands in the air as though I'm going to interrupt his moment of amusement. "I thought you were smarter than me?"

I narrow my eyes, not following along.

"I mean, you have to be fully clothed, and she can't complain about staying here? Come on. You might as well just call a truce and fuck each other silly until those babies are born."

Cam's mind usually drifts to sex or women if it isn't on his family's empire at the fishing docks. He's learning the ropes there, and I heard a rumor last week that his dad is considering retiring and leaving it all to Cam within the next couple years.

"It's not like that."

"What? You don't want to bang her because she's pregnant? Don't tell me you're one of those idiots who thinks your kid is being poked in the head by your dick."

That visual alone spurs me to squirm in the chair. "Thanks for the visual. No. I'd fuck her if it wouldn't destroy us. We're clear that we want different things. She wants me to be a white knight and I only want sex."

He nods and purses his lips. "This isn't white knight enough for her?" He looks out at the truck and the garage that's half full of her belongings.

"What do you mean?"

He tsks. "I can't believe you were in AP classes in high school, and I wasn't. You really can't see what you're doing?"

"She and the babies are my responsibility. I messed up and got her pregnant."

"And you wanted to put her up at your house even before the water damage at her apartment. I'm not sure if you're trying to be her white knight or you just want to control her. Either way, I see a delirious happily ever after in the future for the both of you."

"How do you figure?"

"You're not a white knight. We both know that. You hide your feelings, your hurt. Hell, you're still mourning your mom. And you want to dictate what she does—"

"That's only because—"

He's quick to cut me off. "I know. You want to control it because you can't stand the idea of anything bad happening to someone you care about, but that woman—hell, any woman—doesn't want to be told what to do."

I think about what he's saying. "Since when do you give advice about relationships? You've never even been in one."

"Hey, I dated that Deana chick for, like, four months."

I quirk an eyebrow that he can even keep a straight face. He'd just returned from college, and she was working here during tourist season. She was a summer fling at best. "Whatever. What suggestion do you have?"

"Honestly?"

"No, shithead. Lie to me. Yes! I'm lost and you're here, so I guess it's your guidance I'm willing to take."

"Calm down a little. It's only been, like, what? A couple weeks?" He pushes up off the couch because we still have half a truck to unload into here. "I get that you guys were kind of friends before, but you're in each other's lives forever now. You need to become real friends."

As we walk back to the U-Haul, I think he might actually have a point. Damn, Cam knowing what the hell he's talking about? Who would've thought? But I do need Allie to trust me, and I can't force that upon her. I can't force us to have a bond, so we'll respect one another while raising our kids.

"Let's go, boys! Back to work!" Dori claps her hands.

I roll my eyes, grabbing a box off the truck. As I bring it

to the garage, I catch Allie sitting on the stairs of the porch, talking with my grandma. Our eyes lock and my heart hiccups.

If we're going to be friends, I need to tame this attraction, and that means no more putting my arms around her and telling her how sexy she is. Hard as that may be.

AFTER DORI AND ETHEL LEAVE, Cam following behind to make sure they get to the rental place in one piece, my cell phone rings.

"Greene," I answer.

"Sam Klein's wife just called," Peterson, one of the officers from the station, says.

I look at Allie, who's sitting in front of the television, her head leaned on the back of the couch, eyes shut. I was going to pay her back with a foot rub. One I think she could probably use based on how tired she is. But Peterson wouldn't have bothered to call me unless something big is going down, even if Sam is the mayor.

"What's up?"

"I'm here now and Mindy's screaming and yelling, tossing all his stuff out of the house." I sigh. Mindy is Sam's wife. "She says the Netflix hijack wasn't real, that he filed a false police report and that he really gave the log-on to his girlfriend in Anchorage."

I blow out a breath, pissed off. Sam Klein is the mayor. This isn't going to go smoothly. I trust my guys to handle it, but as the sheriff, I have no choice but to go oversee the situation.

"The crowd is growing," Peterson adds when I don't say anything for a second.

"I get your point. I'm on my way." I tuck my phone in my pocket.

As I'm about to sit to gently wake Allie, her eyes pop open.

"You have to go?" Her voice is groggy.

I nod. "Sam Klein. His wife... it's a long story. I'll be back as soon as I can, but it will be late. I won't be able to give you that foot rub I promised." I frown.

Her understanding smile pierces something inside me. Not many women are cool when plans change at the last minute, but that's my life as sheriff. Although we're not dating, this won't be the last time I have to cancel plans or leave her to go handle a problem.

"It's okay, Fisher. Go."

"I'll be back as—"

She laughs. "I said it was okay. Just go."

I rise off the couch and head upstairs to put my uniform back on. A few minutes later, I say goodbye and I'm out the door.

Sam Klein lives closer to downtown, so once I get to the neighborhood, almost everyone who lives in the vicinity is out of their houses and looking on. I put my siren on to keep the kids on the sidewalk and try to ward people off, so they'll mind their own business, but it won't work. We live in Sunrise Bay after all.

I find Peterson trying to calm Mindy Klein and Sam shoving his belongings into black plastic bags. Mindy tries to get by Peterson, pointing and swearing at her husband.

"Here I thought this was a boring town," Jed says from the street where he stands with Molly and Emilia.

"Don't you have anything better to do?" I say to him, but I catch Cade and Presley walking down the street to join them.

"Nope." He takes out the lollipop he's sucking on and gives me a shit-eating grin.

I head up the walkway. "Mindy, let's take this inside."

She whips her head around and glares at me. "Why? I don't care who knows what scum my husband is. He's been seeing some twenty-five-year-old in Anchorage. You need to arrest him, Fisher. He filed a false police report."

Sam looks exhausted. He's wearing a pair of white briefs and a white T-shirt like he was sleeping when all this started to go down. He must be freezing.

Mindy grabs her phone and pulls up something on the screen. "See? Here it is. Where he gave her our password."

She shoves it into my hand, and I look to see. Sure enough, he did give his password to someone else when he told us he hadn't when we came to investigate after Mindy's call.

Peterson raises both eyebrows at me. We need to do something. We both know it. We can't sweep a false police report under the rug. Even if this seems more like a domestic problem.

"Sam, why don't you dig some clothes out of that bag so we can head to the station?"

"You're kidding me, right?"

This is where things get weird. I've known Sam Klein since I was a boy, and now he has to respect me as the sheriff and not the boy he once watched on Friday nights at the football field. "Please, Sam."

He sighs and digs through the bag. "The house is in my name. I want her out."

The sound of the crowd behind me grows. I'm sure they're filming and taking pictures because that's what we have to deal with in this day and age.

"Peterson, control the crowd. I'll handle this." He walks

away as I step closer to Mindy. "I'm going to take him to the station, but I don't want to leave you alone. Do you have someone you can call?"

As soon as I'm done asking, a car pulls into the neighbor's driveway. Mindy's sister, Julie, runs across the lawn to her.

"We always knew he was a piece of shit." Julie puts her arm around her sister and Mindy sobs.

Thank goodness their kids are grown and off to college. I hope these videos and pictures never reach them.

"Go inside, Mindy. I'll be in touch," I say.

Julie nods, and with her arm around Mindy, they walk up the steps, Mindy's wails echoing in the crisp night air.

"You ready?" I say to Sam, pissed off that he couldn't keep his dick in his pants.

I don't have any respect for guys like Sam. Don't commit if you think you can't be faithful. It's as simple as that. He just threw his entire life away for a girl who's likely not going to be with him long term. How does that make any sense?

I put my hand on Sam's arm and escort him down the walkway, his chin tucked into his chest, trying not to be photographed. No one says anything, but the silent judgment is felt all around as I place him in the back of Peterson's car and shut the door.

"I'll meet you at the station," I tell Peterson.

He nods and slides into his car, squawking his siren to get the bystanders out of the way.

I climb into my truck, taking one last glimpse at Mindy through the window of the house. She's bent over at the waist, her sister barely holding her up. That's just another reason I don't commit—I can't imagine breaking someone like that.

Chapter Twelve

Allie

Fisher comes down on Sunday morning, dressed in jeans and a sweatshirt with a soccer team name on it.

I'm busy at the kitchen table, paying bills and figuring out how I'll manage once the babies arrive. We'll need childcare since I want to—and have to—continue working.

"Good morning," he says, grabbing a to-go coffee cup and filling it. "Thanks for making coffee. I should've been up an hour ago." He shifts over to the pantry and grabs a protein bar.

"I would've woken you had I known."

Ever since Dori and Ethel brought my stuff over, Fisher has been more distant, but respectful. We coexist like roommates. I'm not sure if I've done something to offend him or what. But I'm worried that him deciding to have me move in was a knee-jerk reaction he's regretting at this point.

"It's my fault for staying up and playing video games last night. I just needed downtime."

I shut my laptop, mostly because I don't want him to see where I stand on financials. I've always been a saver, so I'll be okay for a while, but as soon as we're paying childcare, I'm worried about what will happen.

"Well, have fun wherever you're going." I sip my coffee.

"Rylan has a soccer game. I rarely get to go lately, so I said I would drive him there so I could be there during warm-ups."

"You don't owe me an explanation."

"I know. It's just…" He crumples up the wrapper of his protein bar and shoves it in the trash. "Would you want to come with me? Do you have to work?"

"It's my day off." I look at my closed laptop. It would be nice to turn off my brain for a day, rather than spending it obsessing over how much my life is about to change in a few months. "But I would never intrude. I'll be fine here."

"When is the last time you did anything that wasn't working or just hanging around here?"

"I get out."

Am I really that transparent that he can tell I don't have much of a life? I've even shied away from Stella lately because I know she doesn't get a lot of time with her family and I don't want to take away from what little time she does get.

He goes over to the coat rack by the back door and picks mine off the hook. "Let's go." He opens it and holds it out for me. "You're going to a youth soccer game, but I promise you're going to love it."

I stand from the table, thankful I already showered earlier. My hair is pulled up in a messy bun, but my makeup is on and I'm actually dressed in a new pair of maternity jeans and cute T-shirt that says, Make it a Double #twinmom. At this point, I might as well own this pregnancy.

I shrug on my coat, and since it won't zip, I leave it open as if I'm making a fashion statement during the fall in Alaska.

Fisher looks down at where my belly protrudes. He's

smart and knows that there's no way it's zipping up. "You need a new coat."

I glance down. "I get hot anyway." I shrug.

He stares at it for a long time, and I wait for him to argue with me. To say we're stopping on the way to find me one, or worse, put me in one of his. But his gaze lifts to mine and he turns away, opening the back door for me.

I grab my purse from the hanger and walk out, biting my lip to stop my smile. Maybe I've beaten him down and he's not going to boss me around our entire time together. But I'll admit, it's freezing this morning and I want to go back inside the house immediately.

He's a gentleman, opening my door, helping me climb in, and securing the door shut. We drive over to his dad and Marla's to grab Rylan. Fisher exits the truck, opens the front door to the house, and yells to tell his brother he's here. A few seconds later, Rylan pops out of the house, soccer bag slung over his shoulder, and jogs over to the truck. He stops as his hand is about to open up the passenger door.

Climbing into the back seat, he situates himself and puts on his seat belt.

"Hey, Ryguy," Fisher says, looking at him through the rearview mirror. "You remember Allie, right?"

"Hey," he mumbles.

"Hi."

He doesn't talk a lot on the way, his head mostly buried in his phone. He seems like a shy kid based on the couple previous encounters I've had with him. Since Fisher isn't the most talkative either, we end up listening to rock music, which I already knew was Fisher's go-to.

Eventually we pull up to a big sports complex that Stella's husband, Kingston, is half owner of. "You play here?" I ask.

Rylan peeks up from his phone because he must feel me looking over the seat at him. "Yeah."

"You must play with Calista," I say.

"Yeah," he mumbles again and glances at Fisher, opening his door. "I'll see you guys in there."

Fisher chuckles, taking the keys out of the ignition. "He's kind of sensitive when it comes to Calista. Everyone is always razzing him about liking her and stuff. Those two are—"

"Amazing players. They're the best in the area, right? I mean, Rome brags a lot about her. And Jamison…" I shake my head. "I swear this pregnancy is killing my brain cells. How did I not figure out your Rylan is the same Rylan that Jamison's always talking about?"

Jamison is the other owner in the sports complex and is married to Kingston's sister.

"Remember they were at the barbecue?" Fisher's looking at me as though he's concerned about my memory.

"I was a little distracted, and I only saw them in the pool briefly, plus I've never actually met Calista, so I didn't realize that was her. If I remember correctly, you got us out of there pretty quick."

That was the night. The night we created our two little bundles of joy.

"I thought maybe you blacked out or something." He opens his door.

"Sometimes I wish I could forget that night." The truth slips off my tongue faster than a race car, and Fisher's smile drops. "I mean—"

He holds up his hand. "I got it."

Without another glance my way, he climbs out of the truck. I scramble to grab my purse and open the door. The seat belt tightens around me as a reminder that I forgot about it. I fiddle to release it, and I slide out of the truck. He's at the back waiting for me, hands pushed into his pockets.

"You have it all wrong. Why I wish I could forget—"

His eyes drop to my stomach. "I understand fine. Come on, I'll buy you a pretzel."

He dismisses me and a boiling anger only he seems to be able to ignite flares to life.

"Fisher. Stop!" I yell after him.

A man and his son glance over, then continue walking toward the entrance.

Fisher turns around, walks steadily to me, and lowers his head to my ear. "You don't owe me an explanation."

I press my open palm to his mouth to shut him up for once. "Will you please just listen to me?"

He mumbles something, and I tighten my hand.

"If I take my hand off, will you be quiet and just listen to me?"

His whiskey eyes sink into mine and I have no idea if he's going to listen, but I take my hand off because I do not need reports of us arguing outside a kids' sports facility on Scandals of Sunrise Bay.

"It's not that I regret this." I run my hand over my belly. "It's that I can't stop feeling you inside of me." My face heats as though I just bent down in front of an oven.

One side of his lips tip in a cocky grin.

"Yes, Fisher, I can't stop feeling your hands and remembering the feel of you between my legs, okay? So there."

I brush my shoulder against his as I walk past, but he snags my hand at the last second before I'm out of reach. He tugs me into him gently, and my hands splay on his chest. When he tucks an errant chunk of hair that's come out of my bun behind my ear, my breath shakes.

"You think you're alone in that? You're not. But I'm trying

to respect your boundaries." His jaw flexes when he presses his teeth together.

I tip my head back to look up at him. "It will only complicate an already complicated situation."

"But if we both know the score beforehand..."

"Are you really suggesting a friends with benefits relationship with your knocked up one-night stand?"

He frowns. "There are nights I lie awake and wish I would've called you right after our night together. That I would've had you all over my house, because then maybe I wouldn't still want you as much as I do."

My entire core tingles and heats like an uncontrollable fire. There's no putting it out until Fisher is deep inside me. I place my hand on his chest. "I'm not you. You can separate sex and feelings; I'm not sure I can." Though right now I wish like hell I could.

I turn around and walk into the sports facility. He follows right away because he reaches across to open up the door for me to walk through.

"I have to admit I have no idea what the fuck I'm doing here. I'm sorry if I made you uncomfortable," he says as we walk up to the refreshment stand.

I don't respond because I'm not sure what to say, so he just orders me a pretzel with cheese and two waters.

Since we're a little early, there are only a few parents sprinkled around. We sit in the bleachers in silence, watching Rylan warm up with his team. Jamison's instructing him and Calista in practicing a play.

"Everything seemed so much easier when I was that age," I say.

He tears off a piece of my pretzel and dips it in cheese. "I was a horny fucker at Rylan's age. I can't imagine if I'd known you then. I would've never had the self-control I possess right now."

He might lust after me, but is that something I really want? A fuck buddy for the next who knows how many years? Although it does sound pretty good and Fisher is the best lover I've ever had, my gut tells me I'd end up doing more than just lusting for him.

But since we're talking in hypotheticals, I can at least admit something. "I'd have had a big crush on you at that age. There was always something about the bad boys."

"But you want the bad boy with a heart of gold? A tortured soul you can heal, thinking that would make him want to settle down with you? I hate to break it to you, but those guys don't exist."

His words knock the wind from me. I place the pretzel down next to me, my hunger waning.

"Don't act like you know anything about me," I whisper-shout.

"Allie!" A familiar voice pulls me away before tears well in my eyes.

I look over to find Kingston with Maven in his arms.

"Hey, Kingston." I poke Maven's stomach. "Maven."

She giggles and squirms, so Kingston places her down on the bleacher, then turns his attention to Fisher. "Hey, I'm Kingston. You must be Fisher." He extends his hand, and Fisher shakes it.

"What's up, Fish?" Liam Kelly, Kingston's brother-in-law, comes over, and I glance over my shoulder to find a lot of the Baileys emerging into the sports facility. "We're cheering for the same team today."

They shake hands.

"You know Fisher?" Kingston asks Liam.

"Do you really not recognize all my work?" Liam eyes Fisher's arms and hands.

"That reminds me, I need to book in with you," Fisher says to Liam.

"Sure. What are you thinking?" Liam asks.

Fisher glances my way and back at Liam. "We can discuss it when I get there."

Kingston frowns at me, probably feeling the disconnect between Fisher and me.

"Where's Stella?" I ask.

"She's resting with Maisey. Up all night." He sits down in the row in front of us.

Soon the bleachers are filled with Greenes and Baileys. Usually this would make me happy, but all I want to do is get the hell out of here so I can feel sorry for myself.

Fisher

A few days later, I head to the gym to get my head on straight. My emotions look like the New York City subway map—zigging this way and that, one running over the next.

Nikki's husband, Logan, is in the ring with Gavin Price—the child actor turned Hollywood heartthrob who somehow thinks he wants to live in Alaska now.

I start my workout on the treadmill, my warm-up quickly shifting into a run. Even with my headphones in and "Welcome To The Jungle" by Guns N' Roses blaring in my ears, all I see is the crushing disappointment in Allie's eyes when I told her that her belief was impossible.

Why do I care so much about proving her wrong?

Not getting the relief I need, I stop the treadmill and pull the headphones out of my ears, walking over to the boxing ring. "Logan, when's your next opening?"

He holds up his hand to stop Gavin from kicking him, a snicker of a grin crossing his lips. We've sparred a few times, and I can't lie, it's the best thing to clear my mind. Usually, I end up here after a particularly bad case or a scene from an accident that I can't shake.

"Girl problems?" Logan asks with a knowing glint in his eyes.

I groan. "What the fuck does it matter? Just tell me when you're available."

My patience is worn thinner than a condom. Why was I such an idiot in not returning her phone call? I could've had her out of my system by now even if she was carrying my baby. But that's just an excuse—I wanted to claim her in some way that night. Little did I know I was tying us together forever.

"Give me a half hour. But just a warning, this'll involve me canceling on Nikki, so you can take the punishment."

I roll my eyes. My stepsister can be a lot at times and I'm sure to hear about her displeasure for taking her husband away from whatever they had planned.

A half hour is gonna kill me, so I do what I do best. I sit on a stool and talk shit to Gavin.

"So tell me, Gavin, why does some heartthrob actor from Los Angeles want to be this far north?"

Logan glances over and Gavin gets a quick jab into his padded helmet.

"I just wanted out of that town." Gavin's breath is labored.

"You know the entire town of Sunrise Bay knowing your business can be just as bad as LA?"

They separate and jog in place. "I don't care what people say about me."

"Everyone cares to an extent." I'm being hard on Gavin because I'm pissed off with myself and in a lousy mood. It's time I get my head on straight.

"You're in my industry long enough, you get used to it."

"But here you are, hiding out in small-town Alaska."

Gavin stops bouncing from foot to foot and glares at me over his shoulder. Logan slides Gavin's feet out from under him and he falls to the mat.

"You done now?" I ask.

Gavin gets back on his feet. "I have fifteen minutes left."

I nod, impressed that he's not taking the out. Maybe he has a fighting chance in this town. "Did you know you just about ran over my sister a few months ago?"

"Fisher, why don't you do some cardio while you wait?" Logan says, clearly sick of my bullshit.

I'm sure Logan doesn't want to tell me to go fuck myself because he's married to my sister, but I deserve it. I have a lot of respect for Logan. He changed his whole way of life when he retired from MMA and moved up here with Nikki. Now they have the baby.

"Nah. I'm good."

"Then play nice," he says.

I stretch out my shoulders while I wait my turn.

I watch him and Gavin spar for fifteen minutes and manage to keep my shitty attitude to myself. The guy is pretty good for being a pretty-boy actor. Chevelle had posters of him up in her room back when she was young. I shouldn't take out my own shit on him, but I'm also the nosy sheriff who wants to know why he wants to be in our town.

"I heard about the mayor stepping down. Your mother-in-law is gonna fill in as mayor now?" Gavin asks Logan.

"Marla was the runner-up in the last election. Originally he wasn't going to run, and now everyone is saying that it's because he was thinking about leaving poor Mindy for his sidepiece. Not sure what changed, but he ended up running." Logan fills Gavin in on the local gossip.

"You should listen to Nikki's Scandals of Sunrise Bay. Logan's wife will make sure you're up on all the gossip." I offer advice I'm sure Gavin doesn't want. Maybe I'm still annoyed at him for running Posey off the road a few months back.

"I try not to believe everything I hear and read. So much of it is bullshit." He nods at me. "Except I did hear you're expecting twins. Congratulations."

"Thanks."

"Allie's really nice."

My gaze flies to him and my body buzzes with negative energy, like a swarm of wasps are stinging me all over. "You know Allie?"

"I met her the other day at the bookstore. She was picking up some things from Presley." Seems Gavin's making himself right at home here.

"Yeah, my sister-in-law runs a great shop." I ignore the comment about Allie. Well, almost. My fists are clenched so tight they could be nutcrackers.

Logan chuckles under his breath, but when I cut him a look, he tries to tamp it down but barely succeeds.

They finish up and do some lame man-handshake thing.

"Thanks, Loge." Then Gavin waves to me.

I only nod in return.

Once Gavin Price is out of the gym, Logan shakes his head at me. "Could you be more of an asshole?"

My lips press in a thin line. "I can try."

"He's a good guy. I've known him a long time."

"Are you sure he's not just an opportunist?" My skeptical side shines through.

"Opportunist?"

"You were a famous MMA fighter when he met you, right? Now he's moved up to the town you live in. Sounds a little *Single White Female*-ish to me." I shrug and put on my headgear and gloves before sliding through the ropes.

"He's a friend." Logan gives me a side-eye. "You gotta stop thinking the worst of people."

"I'm the sheriff. Of course I think the worst of people. I see them at their worst every day."

We circle one another in the ring. "You know some people find sparring like therapy? They tell me their problems and I give them some insight. Wanna give it a try?"

I huff. "Don't worry about me. I'm not going to cry on your shoulder and lay all my issues at your feet."

Logan swings at me, and I block it. "Maybe you should. You seem to be struggling."

I shake my head and kick him, but he blocks me. Logan's a pretty trustworthy guy. One other time I came in here, I ended up telling him how I couldn't get the vision of an accident scene out of my head. I didn't go into how it reminded me of losing my mother. How I had to have the kids picked up by social services, and the moment I saw the little boy crying while he fought to get free from another officer, it was like I was back on that frozen lake where my mother died. But I did tell him how much it was messing with me.

He's never said another word to anyone that I'm aware of. So I guess he could give me some advice as long as I keep in mind that he married a stranger in Vegas and chased her up here to Alaska.

"It's Allie."

He chuckles and lands a punch to my head. "You did look like you wanted to strangle Gavin with your bare hands when he brought her up."

"I didn't. I just don't like the guy. He's flashy. I'm not."

"He grew up in Hollywood. What do you expect?"

I shrug and we circle one another again. "I'm all over the place. One minute my balls are blue from wanting her so bad, and the next I'm telling her she's delusional to believe in true love."

Logan nods but says nothing.

"I don't want to be the jerk who pops her balloon. Maybe she should believe in that. Hell, maybe she'll find her dream guy someday. The one who wants the family, kids, the wife, and the white picket fence. I'm just not him. She was dealt a shitty hand when I was the one who got her pregnant. With twins." I roll my eyes.

"So you want her to find someone else?"

His words feel like a lash on my skin, but I can't be selfish about this. "I want her to be happy."

"But when Gavin complimented her, you wanted to kill him." He kicks and I block. He's going easy on me.

"That douche can't be my kid's stepfather."

Logan laughs and steps back, bouncing on his feet. "Why not?"

"Because my son and daughter aren't gonna be raised by some Hollywood heartthrob."

He nods and I swing a punch to get the smirk off his face.

"It's not like you wouldn't be in their lives. You just wouldn't be with Allie," he says.

"Exactly, which means I'd have to split time. I may not have wanted kids, but you can be damn sure now that I'm having them, I'm going to be the best dad possible. I think it just makes sense that I should get to approve of whoever she marries."

He stops for a minute and laughs, bending over at his waist. "Seriously? Sometimes I think you time warped in from the caveman era."

"I'm just being honest. If everyone was honest, maybe this world would be a better place."

"Maybe," he says with disbelief in his tone.

We continue circling one another. A few fists here, a kick there, but he's not going nearly as hard as I want him to.

"Have you ever thought of dating her yourself?" His voice is quiet, as though he's worried I'm going to forget the sparring and really want to go at it.

"I don't do relationships."

"Right. But you're struggling to get Allie out of your head."

"It's just about sex, man." I go to get him in the stomach, but he blocks and backs up.

"You sure about that?" He does some fancy move and I back up, lose my footing and end up on the ropes.

I come off the ropes and move toward him. "Of course I am."

"Is it possible you assume it's lust because you've never felt like this for any other woman before? Maybe you do want to date her. I'm not saying you don't wanna fuck her, but did you ever consider that you might also like her as a person?"

I pause from shifting my weight from one foot to the next to think about what he's saying. "You think what I'm feeling isn't just sexual frustration?"

"When was the last time you wanted someone like Allie? That you came in to get rid of some excess energy to quiet your brain? I haven't known you that long, but I'm pretty sure the answer is never."

I cross my arms. "I like that she's carrying my babies, as strange as that is. It gives me this weird feeling."

Logan laughs. "That's normal."

"Are you sure? All I want to do is touch her stomach, and if she'd let me talk to them, I would."

Logan grabs a water and downs half the bottle in one gulp. "I was always kissing and touching Nikki's stomach when she was pregnant. There's a sense of pride that you're bringing new life into the world. I get it."

"But what if I'm mixing up the feelings inside me? What if my attraction to Allie is only because she's carrying my babies?" I sit down and take off my headgear and gloves.

"You do what everyone else does. You figure it out by dating her, by spending more time with her."

We've shared a few meals together and she came to Rylan's game, but I was a bit of an asshole that day, and she was quiet, talking more to Kingston Bailey than to me.

"I don't want to lead her on."

Logan sits beside me, both of our legs hanging over the edge of the ring. "You don't have to tell her that's what you're doing. Don't sleep with her, but take her out. Do things together. Talk to her stomach—with her permission obviously. Do fun things together and see what happens. Either you'll become friends again, or your feelings will grow. I went on pure gut instinct when I married Nikki, but after I came up here and we started spending time together, I figured out I wanted her more than my MMA career, so here I am."

"And you're happy?"

He claps me on the shoulder. "Very."

The door of the gym opens, and Nikki stands there with her hands on her hips. "What the hell, Logan?"

He slides out under the ropes. "Fisher needed a quick fix."

She throws her arms in the air. "You're not a therapist." She walks farther into the gym. "We have about an hour before Mom brings Noah home. Get a move on."

I can't help but chuckle. What a great guy to delay sex with his wife to talk to me.

"Let's go." He swings a bag over his shoulder.

"What's your problem?" Nikki asks me, but I don't want

to tell her anything for fear it will end up on her morning radio show.

"Nothing."

She scoffs. "Imagine having problems when you got someone you don't know pregnant with twins." Her words are thick with sarcasm.

"You're judging me after you married a stranger in Vegas?" I say to her back.

"Touché. Now I'm going home to have sex. Too bad you can't say the same." She gives me a cheeky grin and I roll my eyes.

"See you later, man." Logan gives me a handshake and follows his wife out of the gym.

I sit there with my forehead on the ropes, thinking that he's right. It's about time I get to know the mother of my unborn children better than I do. Maybe I'll like what I find.

Allie

I down two Tylenol after my shift ends because my feet and back ache. On my way out, I wave to Helen, thankful I have tomorrow off to recoup. I'm not sure how much longer I'm going to be able to work, but thankfully Stella hasn't put me on bed rest yet. I understand how high-risk twins can be, but I'd like to continue working as long as I can.

The doors open when I scan my ID card, and I find Fisher sitting in the same chair he was in the night he found out he was going to be a father.

"Fisher? What are you doing here?"

He smiles, and it reminds me of the smiles he gave me before we ever slept together. At the time, I thought that maybe, just maybe, I'd snag a man like Fisher Greene for myself. Until we got to know each other better and I discovered he didn't ever want to get married or have a family. I'll deny it forever, but he's right—a small part of me thought I could change that about him. So foolish.

"Hey, you hungry?" He's still in his uniform, so I assume he must've gotten caught up working tonight.

"If this is your way of making sure I get home okay, don't bother." I walk through the emergency room and out the sliding glass doors.

He catches up quickly because he has long legs and he's not carrying two bowling balls in his stomach. "It's not. I just thought maybe you'd want to grab something to eat. Like we used to."

I stop and turn toward him. The Alaska fall air chills me since I'm in scrubs and a sweatshirt. "The Greywall diner?"

He nods and runs a hand through his hair. I'd almost say he looks nervous, like he has something to tell me and he's not looking forward to it.

"Just tell me now," I spit out, not in the mood for him to schmooze me through dinner just to drop a bomb. Has he met some girl he wants to screw? Or maybe he wants me out of the house already?

He shakes his head adamantly. "I have nothing to tell you."

I cock my hip to the side and cross my arms. "We don't do eating at three in the morning anymore, Fisher. We eat dinner at your place... sometimes. We talk almost never. So tell me what this is all about because I'm tired and cranky. Pancakes sound really good, and I don't want you to ruin pancakes for me."

He chuckles and shrugs off his sheriff's jacket. Stepping forward, he lays the coat over my shoulders.

"Don't do nice things!" I yell because I'm flustered, and my hormones are making my moods swing more than an all-star major league baseball player.

Another light chuckle floats out of him. "I honestly just wanted to take you to eat. I promise I won't ruin pancakes for you."

My defenses ease when I see kindness in his features. That, and the fact that all I'm thinking about is butter melting over a stack of pancakes and syrup dripping off each one. "Fine."

I stomp toward my car where, surprise surprise, I find his truck is parked next to mine.

"I'll drive," he says.

"No. I'll meet you there."

He narrows his eyes. "Allie, we live in the same house. I can bring you back tomorrow to get your car."

"Fine." I walk over to the passenger side, and he opens the door for me. I climb up on the step and hoist myself in, which is becoming harder but is a lot easier than driving. I shoo away his hand. "I have it." I reach forward and shut the door.

He rounds the front of the truck and gets in the driver's seat. We drive in silence, which is fine by me. I lay my head back and close my eyes for a moment, being lulled by "Wild Horses" by The Rolling Stones floating from the speakers.

We get on the highway for the brief drive to the neighboring town that has the only twenty-four-seven diner around. It's like a spotlight in a dark sky when we pull off the highway.

After he parks his truck, he turns off the ignition but remains in his seat.

"I'm sorry, Allie," he whispers, like he wants me to hear but maybe not himself. I'm sure for someone like Fisher, apologizing isn't easy.

"For what?"

He licks his lips. "For being an asshole to you at Rylan's game. I have no explanation other than I felt judged. I didn't want you thinking..." He shakes his head as though he's trying to scramble his thoughts into order. "I mean, I am who I am, and I'm not sure I believe that anyone truly ever changes, but there's no reason I had to act like you were stupid for believing in something I don't."

Was that a hint of hesitation in his eyes, as though he

might be rethinking his beliefs about marriage? I inwardly reprimand myself. He's right—rarely do people change their core beliefs.

"It's okay, Fisher. I fully understand who I'm getting with you." I put my hand on his and squeeze. "Now, I'm starving. Let's eat."

I climb out of his truck, and he joins me at the front a second or two later. He doesn't say anything else, and though his words hurt me, he was truthful and that's all I expect from him.

We're seated at a table that faces the parking lot. I don't even look at the menu before ordering pancakes, an herbal tea, and a glass of milk for some calcium. Fisher orders a burger, no fries, but adds a chocolate milkshake.

"You do know the milkshake is probably worse than the fries?"

He shrugs. "I need calcium too."

I chuckle and situate my napkin just so, then I grab the tin of creamers to stack them.

"This again?" he asks.

I did the same thing our very first time here. The awkwardness of the moment makes me want to distract myself. I put them all back in the bowl and shove it close to the salt and pepper shakers.

"It's okay if you want to do it."

I shake my head. "No, it's fine. So how was work tonight?"

"Nothing too eventful. The Kleins are divorcing. She retracted her statement about him falsifying a police report and said that it was her who made the changes on their account." He looks over his shoulder—I assume to make sure no one is eavesdropping, but it's the middle of the night and we're the only ones seated in our area. "I think they came to some kind of agreement, and she had to drop it."

"All that paperwork for nothing."

"Right?" He grins. "That's the only reason I care. I could've told Mindy that's what was going to happen."

"Why?" I tilt my head.

"Mindy's never had to work. It's noble, all the volunteering she's done around the community, but that's not the kind of experience most employers look for on a résumé. So her ability to support herself wouldn't have many options, plus who knows if she even wants to work after not doing so all these years. She's never brought any income into the home, and nine times out of ten, the men eventually think of it as all theirs—the money, the assets they've bought with their money—and it becomes an arguing point in a divorce. That's why that little girl inside your stomach is going to find a career and a passion so she never has to rely on a man."

I cover my belly in a loving rub. "I agree, but I'm shocked to hear that come out of your mouth."

His milkshake and my tea and milk come. I steep the tea and let it cool while drinking my glass of milk.

He pounds his straw on the table to free the straw from the wrapper. "You think I'm that controlling, huh?"

I hold up my hands. "You're the one who says you're controlling."

"I want you safe, but I don't want to take things away from you."

"Just my freedom to drive or the ability to live where I want," I joke.

His smile dips down. "You really think that?"

I laugh at his serious expression. "I'm not sure what I think, Fisher. We were just getting to know one another when we slept together, then you never returned my phone call. You see me five months later, pregnant, and immediately you're demanding that I move in with you."

"Fair enough," he says, then his eyes rise to meet mine. "I'd never tell you not to work or stop you from doing something you wanted to do. I just might want to go with you."

"You mean act as a bodyguard at work with me?" I imagine him sitting in that chair during my entire shift.

"No. It's hard to explain... I never thought I was like that until you said you were pregnant. I mean, I knew I like to have control over things, but not people."

"So I'm the lucky one?" I raise an eyebrow.

The food arrives and acts as a great distraction. I don't want to get into it with Fisher, so I spread the butter and watch it melt on the pancakes, then I grab the syrup and pour it over top. I glance up and notice Fisher isn't setting up to eat.

I set down the syrup and his hand lands on mine. His dark gaze is solely on me, and it's unnerving. My heart thumps against my chest wall like a drum.

"When my mom died, it changed me—forever." His voice comes out rougher than sandpaper.

I sit back in my seat, watching for a minute before he continues to speak.

"Have you heard the story already?" he asks. I think maybe a part of him wishes I have so he doesn't have to retell it.

I shake my head and he nods.

"My dad, Cade, Xavier, Adam, and I were all at football practice. Chevelle was at home with Mom. Chevelle fell asleep on the couch before we left—she was five at the time —and Mom was cleaning. We don't know all the specifics because Chevelle was too young and... well, she's the only one who really knows what happened. But at some point Chevelle woke up and wandered out to the pond that's through the forest at the house. We'd ice skate and play hockey out there once it froze over."

My stomach clenches because I know how this story ends—in devastation. He's made remarks about his mom drowning in a frozen lake before. I try to keep my face neutral and not show him how much I'm breaking inside.

"Chevelle always wanted to hang with us, so we figure she probably assumed that's where we were. By the time my mom realized she was gone, we were already returning home. My mom ran through the woods and my dad barely got the truck in park before he ran after her. I guess he saw the fear in my mom's eyes." He sucks in a breath. "By the time we all got to the lake, my mom was on the other side, sending Chevelle back to my dad and us boys. She had this smile like she was so relieved she'd made it before something happened to her little girl. I remember she let out a huge exhale and my dad shared the same relief as Chevelle came to safety off the ice." He swallows and his Adam's apple bobs.

"You don't have to finish, Fisher," I tell him, but it's like I didn't even speak.

"The ice cracked and splintered, and her smile of relief shifted to fear. It all happened so fast. I swear her scream rattled the trees as she went down, a dishcloth still in her hands."

He pauses for a long moment. I'm sure it's like he's back there, reliving his mother's death. His jaw clenches and tics. "Cade ran to call 911. My dad managed to get her out, but she was in there too long. The ambulance came, but she couldn't be saved."

I slide out of my side of the booth and into his side.

We're not a couple, and he's not the type of guy who likes comfort, especially in public, but I'm not the type of woman not to comfort someone who needs it.

I wrap one arm around his shoulder and half hug him as best I can. "I'm so sorry, Fisher."

He nods into my neck. "Everyone always is. But you should know what happened because it made me who I am today." He eyes my stomach and meets my gaze. "I already love them so much, and that feeling scares the shit out of me. I know what it's like to lose someone you love that much."

A tear slips down my cheek and I brush it away. I take his hand and place it on my belly. "It's amazing, right? How do we love them this much when we haven't even seen them?"

His hand runs along my stomach like a warm hug. "I'll try to loosen up."

I place my hand over his and link our fingers. "And I'll give you some slack."

We sit in the booth side by side like two high schoolers who can't keep their hands to themselves, and for the first time, it feels like we're a team.

Chapter Fifteen

Fisher

$\mathcal{I}$t's Friday night, which in Sunrise Bay during the fall means high school football. All three of my brothers and I played quarterback. Tonight though, the school is honoring Xavier, who flew in for one night to get his award before he has to fly back out so he's ready to play Chicago on Sunday.

I asked Allie to come with me to the game because I'm trying to do what Logan suggested—get to know her better, build our friendship back up. I didn't anticipate that meant that I'd divulge my entire childhood sob story, but for some reason, I wanted her to know I wasn't being a jerk and trying to get her to do my bidding in a possessive, controlling way.

I park the truck and pull out two blankets, then we each put on our hats and mittens.

"If you're too cold, let me know and we can leave," I tell her.

"No way. This is your brother's big night. I run like an oven lately anyway. Don't let me go streaking across the field."

I look down and she's smiling at me.

"I'm kidding, Fisher."

I lean in and whisper, "I know, but I wouldn't be opposed to it."

Her cheeks are the color of pink rose petals, and I'm fairly sure it's from what I said and not the crisp wind whipping at us. It's the first sexual comment I've made since talking to Logan and I'm glad she was semi responsive to it.

"Well, I'm sure other people would. Besides, you haven't seen me naked for a month so..."

I place my hand on her growing belly. Since that night at the diner, she's yet to push me away. The other day I convinced her to let me play some rock music for them. So the little ones heard "November Rain" by Guns N' Roses, then we talked about the iconic nine-minute music video and why Slash walks out of the church to play a guitar solo and whether or not she really did die.

"Don't underestimate the power you have over me."

The pink in her cheeks deepens and she turns away from me. I have the urge to place my finger under her chin and bring her face to mine, but a limo pulls up beside us. The crowd ohs and ahs as it stops in front of the entrance to the field.

"Check this guy out." Cam comes over, thumbing at the limo. "Like his five-year deal didn't just set records, he's gotta show us all up by arriving in a limo?" I laugh, and Cam bangs on the roof. "Come on out, pretty boy."

Cam's ridden Xavier ever since he went pro, busting his balls for every commercial Xavier's in. Every time Xavier slides to stop from being tackled, Cam texts him to tell him that he's growing soft. I have my suspicions that Cam wanted to try to go pro at some point—he was a great wide receiver during our time here—but he knows where his commitment lies. He always has.

The door of the limo opens, and a set of toned, slender legs slides out.

Cam and I look at each other. What the hell is going on?

A tall, willowy woman with long blonde hair exits the limo. There are many things wrong with this picture. The first being that she's wearing a skirt and heels to an Alaskan high school football game. The second is that her boobs are about to pop out of her top. Maybe the thick layer of makeup she's wearing will keep her face warm, but everything else is going to freeze off.

"Allow me to introduce myself." Cam steps closer with his hand extended.

"Talk about self-esteem crusher," Allie mumbles.

I lower my hand until I secure my gloved one to her mitten. If anything, to convey I'd rather have her than this woman who looks like I could break her in two.

The mystery blonde looks at Cam the way I assume she does a Snickers bar. With disdain.

Cam retracts his hand when she doesn't shake it. "All right then."

We don't have to wait even a minute before Xavier steps out wearing a three-piece suit, his hair styled to perfection.

"What the fuck?" Cam says what I'm thinking.

Where the hell is my baby brother with unruly blond hair and a permanent five o'clock shadow? This styled-to-perfection man in front of me can't be him.

"Hey, boys," Xavier says with a bright smile. He shakes Cam's hand, then mine. "Allie, right?"

"Um... yeah. Hi."

He inches forward and kisses her cheek before placing his hand on her belly. "I heard about my little niece and nephew. Are they all snug in there?"

Allie looks to me to answer because I think she's probably wondering why his hand is on her stomach. Then again, Allie's pretty laid back.

I slap my brother's arm. "Don't touch a pregnant lady's belly unless you ask first."

"Whoa!" Xavier steps back, his hands in the air. "I heard about that protectiveness. He's like a damn lion with his pack." He directs that statement to the woman he brought. His arm slides around her waist and he tugs her to him. "This is Giulia... Giulia, this is my brother, Fisher, his best friend Cam, and Fisher's... Allie."

"You can call me his baby mama," Allie says with a roll of her eyes.

"You gonna have them soon?" Giulia asks with what might be an Italian accent.

Cam's mouth is still hanging open, trying to process this.

I look around for Clara because I can't help but wonder what her reaction will be. Xavier has never brought a woman home before.

"I'm having twins. They still need to cook a little longer," Allie responds.

The woman's eyes bulge out. "You have stretch marks?"

"Um..." I give Xavier a look to signal to get this woman out of here before I say something I won't regret, but he might.

"We should go, Giulia. Want some hot chocolate?" Xavier puts his hand on the small of her back and leads her away.

"That's not gonna warm her up," Cam says to their backs, and Xavier puts up his middle finger as they walk away. Cam breaks the small distance between us, leaning into Allie and me. "What's going on? How does your brother get ass like that?"

"I thought he and Clara are a couple?" Allie whispers.

I shake my head. "Just best friends."

"I'm not so sure about that." She tugs on my arm and points toward the parking lot.

A stunned Clara is standing outside her car, her eyes on Xavier and Giulia talking to someone just inside the fence line around the track.

"Clara!" Cam screams and I punch his shoulder. "What?"

Then Xavier turns as though he heard Cam and looks out at the parking lot.

"Oh my god," Allie whispers.

"What?" I ask softly.

"You don't feel it?"

"What are you talking about?" Cam asks.

The three of us are gawking between them as though they're our new reality TV show.

"The tension, the emotion, the anger, the love," Allie says.

Clara and Xavier's eyes are locked for what feels like hours when it must only be seconds. Clara swallows, then Giulia tears Xavier's attention back her way. Clara turns to look at us and we all look down as though we're searching for something we dropped.

"Hey, guys," she says when she approaches. "Oh, you're glowing," she says to Allie with both mitten-covered hands out in front of Allie's stomach. "May I?"

"Sure." Allie glances at me as Clara pretends to not be affected by seeing Xavier with who I'm assuming is a model.

"I can't wait to meet these little ones. How are you feeling?" Clara asks.

"What the hell is going on, Clara?" Cam asks, but she ignores him.

"Hey, guys!" Chevelle bounces up with pigtail braids in

her hair, a pink hat with matching mittens, and a long black coat and boots.

"It isn't negative twenty," Cam says.

"I get cold easily." She secures a blanket in her arms. "How is everyone?"

"Xavier just got here." I nod in the direction where he was last.

Chevelle smiles. "Oh great. Is he staying at your house, Clara?"

Clara finally looks up. "No."

We've all known something happened this summer, but nobody has had the guts to ask what. We suspect Presley, Clara's sister, might know, but I think none of us wants to put her in an awkward position by asking.

"Let's go." I tug on Allie's hand to lead the way.

I pay for us to get in, and we walk along the track toward the bleachers. The stage is already set up for Xavier's big shining moment. We buy hot chocolate and popcorn, then climb the bleachers. A few people say hello and we wave.

Chevelle, Cam, and Clara sit in front of us. Dad and Marla arrive next and sit behind us, and within fifteen minutes, the Greenes have filled this entire section of the bleachers.

"Did you see Xavier?" I ask Cade.

He rolls his eyes. "Think fame has gone to his head?"

"He looks like a *GQ* model instead of a pro quarterback," Jed chimes in.

"Okay, guys, let's give him a break," Dad says behind us, but whatever.

Allie secures her blanket around her, and I do the same with the second one I brought.

"How isn't she blue when she's only wearing an inch of fabric?" Posey asks.

"Fashion over common sense, I suppose," Presley says. Her hand slides out from under her blanket, and she squeezes Clara's knee. She definitely knows whatever the hell it is that's going on.

"Give me some of the blanket?" Cam asks Chevelle.

"Get your own." She slides away from him, but he just slides after her.

I watch them carefully, not thrilled with the flirting tone Cam's using. It's the same one he uses when he wants to get into a girl's pants. I've heard it enough through the years when he's picking up women.

"I'm cold," he whines.

I throw my blanket to Cam, and it hits him on the back of the head. "There."

Cam makes a stink as if I threw a boulder at him.

Chevelle huffs. "It's fine. I'll share."

"Use it, Cam," I tell him through clenched teeth, not asking but ordering.

Allie places her blanket over my legs, sliding closer to me. "We can share."

This leaves us hip to hip, thigh to thigh, and all I want to do is place my hand on her knee and slowly move it up her leg. To tease her core through her jeans. But I stop myself because that's my dick talking, not my brain.

The announcers come on the field, pulling all of our attention to the fifty-yard line. After they announce Xavier, he saunters up there with a swagger he's never had before. Giulia follows him.

I swear Clara growls in front of me. Usually she'd have his number painted on her cheeks and she'd be the one on stage with him.

The detective in me wants to dissect the situation and figure out exactly what happened, but Allie's hand slides to my thigh, distracting me. Without looking at her, I slide my hand under our blanket and put my hand on her thigh.

Something happens in my stomach when she gives my thigh a light squeeze. I haven't had butterflies since I was fifteen years old. Maybe the hot chocolate isn't sitting right.

Chapter Sixteen

Allie

"Why do you want to go to Lamaze?" Stella asks. "I thought we were going to plan a C-section."

The bell rings over the door of The Grind, and we both glance over to see Amy from the Twisted Stem come in and head to the counter.

I turn my attention back to Stella. "Did you even listen to my birthing plan? I want to try natural birth."

"Of course, of course. But you're having twins. That means a C-section."

"What? Women did it for years. There's no reason I can't."

She's silent for a moment, which is so Stella—she wants to make sure she words whatever's going to come out of her mouth correctly. "Do you know how many complications happened back then?"

"Come on, modern medicine has come around." I stir my tea, which turns out is no substitute for my coffee addiction.

"True, and C-sections are part of that modern medicine. Why risk it? We can schedule you out. No stress and you can even pick their birth date." She leans back in her cute blouse and linen pants, one heel hanging off her toes with her legs crossed. She's so put together. If she wasn't my best friend, I might hate sitting across from this classic beauty while I'm wearing leggings and a big sweater with the equivalent of two bowling balls underneath.

"I want the surprise of when my water breaks. The rush to the hospital. Me screaming in pain until I can't take it and beg for drugs. I want to know what it feels like to deliver vaginally."

She blows out a breath, staring at me over the rim of her coffee cup. "You and your wanting everything a specific way."

I sip my tea and it burns my tongue, so I set it on the table to cool down. "What does that mean?"

She tilts her head, and her curls bounce off her shoulder. "You know what it means." Her dark eyes dare me to argue. "You have this idea of how you want things to go, and you have a hard time pivoting away from that dream."

"Should I remind you that I'm pregnant with twins from a one-night stand who doesn't believe in commitment?"

Thankfully, Zoe, owner of The Grind, brings me a warm muffin. Good, I could use the distraction of a treat.

"You're coming in next week for your glucose test." Stella eyes my muffin, probably wondering how many more carbs and treats I've been consuming.

I tear off a chunk and throw it into my mouth, shooting her a "so what?" look.

"That was your doctor talking," she says. "As your friend, I have to say, King said you two were cozy at the soccer game."

What bench was Kingston sitting on? Not mine, because I was giving Fisher the cold shoulder. But I can't deny that things have been different between us for the last week. He touches my belly a lot, and he hardly ever plays his video games when he's home anymore.

"Things are… I have no idea how to explain it." I peek over my shoulder since we're in his town and I don't want anyone to overhear me. "He's being sweet."

"You mean he finally grew up?"

Stella isn't a huge fan of Fisher. Him not answering or returning my phone call really pissed her off, and as my best friend, she's always protective of me. I can't fault her.

"Give him a break," I say.

She sips her coffee and doesn't say anything for a beat. "How is he sweet?"

I smile at that. She's so awesome to put aside her feelings about him. "If I didn't know better, I'd say he's almost interested in me. As a friend of course."

"Friend?"

"A friend who's having his babies?" I phrase it like a question because I have no idea what's in Fisher's head. "He's opened up a lot about his issues."

"His commitment issues."

I wipe my mouth. "Not everyone is Kingston."

A big grin creases her lipsticked lips. When was the last time I wore lipstick? "He is perfect, but he had plenty of issues for a long time."

By the time I met Kingston, he was already all in for Stella. It was their second chance, and he had no plans of letting her slip away again.

"Not the Kingston I know."

"Back to you." Her eyes widen. "What are his issues?"

"Well, his mom died when he was ten."

Her shoulders sink. She understands how the death of a parent at a young age can affect you growing up. She and Kingston share that one disheartening fact.

"That's why he doesn't want to get married?"

I shrug. "I think so. He told me that he loves the babies already and that scares him."

"Has he tried therapy?"

"I don't know, but since he told me about his mom, he almost seems to be trying harder."

"And how do you feel about that?" She leans forward and tears off a piece of my muffin.

I slide the plate to the center of the small table. She puts up her hand, but we both know she'll have another piece. After all, unlike me, she doesn't have a glucose test next week.

"We'll have to co-parent, so it's good that he makes an effort."

"So you don't have feelings for him?" Go figure she hammers me with the one question I'm struggling to answer myself.

The football game, our talks at night, him having the kids listen to his rock music, all the moments we've shared recently, they only endear him to me. He reminds me of the man I thought he was when we started our friendship months ago. Every time he slides his hand in mine, my body hums with electricity, but my heart also warms from the comfort of having someone have my back. But I'm left confused, not understanding what he wants from me.

"It's an easy question, Allie," Stella interrupts my thoughts. I take a chunk of muffin to distract myself and she slides the plate away. "Answer."

Isn't that the problem with best friends? They know when you're stalling.

"I shouldn't have feelings for him," I answer truthfully.

"That doesn't answer the question." She uncrosses her legs, sitting straighter in her chair, elbows on the table.

"I don't know. I…"

Her eyes close and she shakes her head. "I knew I should've moved you in with me." She falls back into her chair as though she's exhausted from handling me.

"Hey, I'm not your eighty-five-year-old grandma," I say. "I can make my own decisions."

She looks concerned when she says, "You've fallen for him."

"No, I haven't."

She shoots me her mom look. The one that orders me to admit the truth.

"I haven't. I know he doesn't want that."

"Listen, you can convince yourself of anything, but you also know it's okay if you do have feelings for him, right? I mean, you're carrying his babies."

I glance out the window and see Presley and Cade sitting on a bench. They're laughing together and Cade bends down and kisses her, making her face light up.

"That's what you want," Stella says softly.

I look at her to see she's followed my vision outside. "I can't deny it. I do."

She clutches my hands. "Then do one thing for me."

My forehead wrinkles. "What?"

Her face grows serious. "Forget the fairy tale BS. Just go with what your heart feels. Don't hold back because it's not exactly how you envisioned this moment in your life being."

"I am," I say, but she shakes her head when I open my mouth.

"I know you, Allie. Instead of just going with whatever is happening between you two, you're second-guessing every-thing. You're thinking it's not right because he didn't court you or hasn't bought you flowers or whatever other fantasies you have in that head of yours."

I shake my head. "It doesn't matter. He doesn't want *that*." I point outside at his brother, and I wonder why he's not terrified by the idea of a relationship. His mother died too.

"People change. They can change and want different things."

"Since when are you Team Fisher?"

She shakes her head. "All I'm saying is I didn't want a muffin when I walked in here and now I can't stop eating yours. Sometimes people don't know what they want until it's right in front of them." Her perfectly arched eyebrows raise, and I laugh.

"You're comparing a muffin craving to Fisher wanting a happily ever after?"

She points at me. "See! Stop thinking in fairy-tale terms. Just enjoy whatever is happening, because I know you and you're already invested. It's too late to lock up your heart at this point."

She finishes my muffin, and I contemplate what she's saying. I hate it when she's right. It's like she's my older sister who's lived through it all before.

"And look at that," she says, glancing out the window.

Fisher is in his uniform, walking across the cobblestone street, and stops to talk to his brother and Presley.

Stella's phone goes off and she picks it up from the table. She's on her feet, shrugging on her coat that perfectly matches her outfit.

"Tell me I'll be as put together as you again at some point in my life," I say.

She places her hand on mine and squeezes. "I promise. I still have ten pounds from Maisey that I want to lose."

Ten pounds, my ass.

She leans down and gives me a hug. "Think about what I

said," she whispers. "And accept that there's a good chance you'll be delivering in an operating room."

We smile at one another because she's going to give me what I want, but Stella also wants to be prepared in case the worst-case scenario happens.

"Love you," I say.

"Love you back."

She walks out of the coffee shop, and I look out the window at Cade and Presley, who are now walking hand in hand into her bookstore. Fisher isn't there anymore, and I kind of hate that I missed him.

I finish off my tea and move to stand, but when I go to tuck in my chair, a hand steadies me on my hip.

"Whoa. Sorry," a deep voice says.

Fisher.

I look over my shoulder and see him right behind me. "Hi."

"Hi."

"How are you?" I ask when he doesn't say anything else.

"I'm good."

I nod. The two of us stand there, not saying a word. I'm not sure why he's here. Did he think I saw him and he just didn't want to walk away because that'd be rude?

"Fisher, you want a drink?" Zoe asks from behind the counter.

"No, I'm good. Thanks, Zoe." He turns briefly and I take it as my opportunity to grab my coat from the back of the chair.

He examines it as I put it on. It's the same coat and I still can't zip it up.

"Do you have to go back to the station?" I ask.

"I had a call down on Turner Road and I wanted to see you after."

I blink and blink again. Is he serious?

"How did you know I was here?" I ask.

He bites the inside of his lip and his telltale smirk, a sign that he did something I'm not going to like, shows itself. "I sensed it?"

I jut out my hip. "Fisher..."

"Why don't we go shopping? Get you some clothes."

"Don't change the subject." I lock my eyes with his to make sure he's telling me the truth.

"You need a new coat." He takes the two sides and stretches them forward to show that they won't cover my belly.

"I need a lot of things."

Like an orgasm.

"Then let's go." He nods toward the door.

"I'm not going anywhere until you tell me how you knew I was here."

He picks up my teacup, Stella's coffee cup, and my muffin plate, turns his back to me, and places them on the counter for Zoe.

"Spill."

He sighs and tries to bite down his smirk—unsuccessfully, I may add. "I may have downloaded one of those tracking apps on your phone." I open my mouth to protest, and he holds up his hands. "What if something happened to you and you couldn't tell me where you were?"

I draw in a deep breath so I can think before I react. The gesture is creepy and sweet at the same time. I know families do it all the time and I would've agreed if he had asked, but he didn't. I am angry, but rather than wage this war with him, I place my hands on his cheeks and stare into his eyes.

"Are you mad?" he asks.

"Yes. Don't do anything like that again. But if it makes

you feel better, I'll leave it on. But once these babies come out, it gets deleted."

"Deal," he says. "Now can I take you shopping?"

"You can go shopping with me. Yes."

His fingers graze down my arm, lightly touching my hand until our fingers are entwined as he leads us out of The Grind as if we're a couple.

Stella's right—it's too late. If I'm truthful, it was too late after we slept together. I'm already falling, and I can't stop myself midflight.

Chapter Seventeen

Fisher

*L*ater that week, we walk into the hospital and Allie takes control since she knows practically everyone here. If someone was made to live in a small town, it's Allie. She's so bubbly and personable, I'm sure people wonder what she ever saw in me enough to sleep with me.

"So this is a breathing class?" I ask when we step into the elevator.

"Lamaze, but really it's just a birthing class. Something to help prepare. Which—" She cringes and touches her stomach.

I cover her hand and step forward. "What?"

"Oh sorry. Nothing. But I was thinking we need to talk about our birth plan. I've communicated to Stella that I want to try for a natural childbirth."

"Does that mean no drugs?" I remember when I was a rookie, a lady went into labor and I was first on the scene. She kept saying not to give her drugs, she wanted to do it naturally. I told her I wasn't a paramedic, so she didn't have to worry about it.

"I'm not opposed to the drugs. I just want to have them vaginally instead of a C-section."

"You want to push them out." My eyes stray to between her legs.

She laughs and lightly pushes me away. "Stop looking at me there."

I've tried to keep all the sexual innuendos at bay, but seriously, the more I'm around her, the more challenging it is to do. I'm struggling not to think about her, but now she just gave me a visual of a baby coming out of there.

Damn it, I really fucked up when I didn't call her back.

"Why?" I ask.

"Why what?"

The elevator pings and the doors slide open. We step out and she turns right while I'm still looking at the signs to tell us where we're going.

"Why would you want to do that? Won't it mess stuff up and be really painful?"

She stops in the middle of the hallway. "It heals, jackass."

"Well, I don't know what happens down there after a woman has a baby..."

She crosses her arms and juts out her hip. I have a habit of pissing her off. "What? What are you worried about, Fisher?"

When she gets this mad, she's like one of those mean older teachers from the movies who would hit you across the knuckles with a ruler. I'm hesitant to tell her what I'm really thinking.

"I'm not worried about anything. I just wonder why you'd want to do that if you had the option not to?"

"It's my vagina and I get to say what happens to it, understand?"

A nurse walks by and glances over her shoulder at us.

"Can you lower your voice?" I whisper.

"It's a hospital. They've heard the word vagina before. Keep talking, Fisher." Her fiery eyes tinge with a hint of pissed off. "You're worried I won't be tight enough after I push out both your babies?"

I raise my hands. "God, no. I don't know how these things work. I just don't like the idea of you in pain."

She steps forward, her hand on my chest, rising to her tiptoes. "Do you think post-op is a euphoric experience?" She tilts her head at me, and yeah, now I feel like an ass. "In the event that your concern does have something to do with the state of my vagina after birth, tell the douchebag inside you that he's an asshole. I'll be healed and just fine should that day ever happen. But if the douchebag side keeps showing his true colors, he'll have nothing to worry about because that day will never come."

She falls back on her heels, and I look at her. "I didn't mean it that way. But you should know that it gets me all hot and horny when you're this riled up."

Her cheeks turn cherry-blossom pink. The color alone makes me wish I could whisk her away and deepen the color until it matches her lips.

"I'm serious. I want to shut you up with my mouth."

Her breath hitches. "Stop it, Fisher. We can't." She stomps off down the hall.

Who am I kidding, I'm not Logan. I can't sit around and wait for her to change her mind about me. I'm not known for my patience. I take her arm and look both ways, opening the door of a janitor's closet.

"What are you doing? We're going to be late." She pushes against my chest.

The light is already on in the small room, and I cage her in against the shelving unit. "I know you feel it. I can tell."

"It doesn't matter what I feel. I'm not getting myself twisted into a pretzel only to end up having to unravel myself from you. We have to co-parent, and sex will only complicate things."

I stare into her eyes, studying the flecks of green inside the hazel and wondering if I should voice what I'm feeling. Once I do, there's no going back. Screw it. "What if I want to explore this thing between us? See if we could be a couple?"

My mother's death might have scarred me and scared me off loving someone for fear of having to deal with a crushing loss, but on the flip side, maybe it also taught me that life is short.

"A couple?" She laughs nervously. "You and me?" She laughs again. "Fisher…"

I hate the way she says my name as if she thinks I've lost all sense. "I'm serious."

"If this is because you're worried about seeing the kids… we'll stay for a while after they're born. I won't be able to do it all by myself anyway. We'll figure it out—"

I crowd her now, my abs pressing gently against her swollen stomach that holds two pieces of me, and my hand slides up to cradle her cheek. I tilt her head to look up at me. "That's not why. I can't do it anymore. Yes, I want you. And maybe it's lust, but I love being around you too. I tried to be friends and take this slow, but I'm not a slow kind of guy. You know that about me. Hell…" My other hand cradles her stomach. "These two wouldn't be here if I took things slow."

Wetness puddles in her eyes. "Fisher… please don't say this just to get inside my pants. We can lift the restrictions, you can go sleep with someone else, but don't play games with me."

I lean in so I'm eye level with her, one hand still on her stomach and the other on her cheek. "I'm not playing games, Allie. I wanna date you."

She laughs and a tear slips free, falling down her cheek before my thumb swipes it away. Our eyes lock.

"I think we're doing everything backward. And you realize I'm growing bigger by the day, right?" She tries to look away from me, but I don't let her. "Are you sure?"

"We're both off in two nights. I'm taking you out."

Her chest heaves up and down.

"Say yes," I whisper.

She nods.

"I need to hear you say it."

"Yes," she whispers back.

"Can I ask one more question?"

"What?"

"Can I have my good-night kiss right now?"

The cutest giggle falls from her lips and her smile lights up. The fact that we're in a janitor closet with the smell of bleach surrounding us doesn't make this my finest moment. But I know it's one I won't forget.

"You really don't work slow, huh?"

I run my hand over her belly in answer to her question.

"Okay," she says.

I bend my neck and she inches up on her tiptoes. My tongue slides along my lips in preparation and my eyes drift closed as I inch closer to her. I glide my hand through the strands of her silky hair, ready to cradle her head while I slip my tongue between her lips.

The door slams open and the neon lights of the hospital hallway puncture the bubble we created.

We break apart. Damn it all to hell.

"This isn't a nightclub," the janitor says with a scowl.

"Sorry! Hormones." Allie touches her stomach. "Even stronger with twins. We're very sorry." She takes my hand and guides me out of the closet.

He just makes a noise as though he's heard that before. Don't nurses and doctors get it on all the time?

"You're already getting me in trouble," she mumbles, but walks a little closer to me.

I untwine my hand from hers and place my arm around her waist, pulling her as close to me as I can. "Sorry, I have that effect."

She tilts her head to lean on my arm and looks up at me. "What kind of sheriff are you?"

"Oh, you'll find out soon enough."

I watch her breasts rise and fall with a deep breath and hope I'm having the same sexual effect on her that she has on me. I'm not sure how much longer I can wait to have her. There's so much I want to do to her, and for the first time in forever, it's not to quench my own sexual desires. Okay, well, I am a man and want mine, but I want to please her until she's limp on the bed with exhaustion after screaming my name.

THERE ARE four other couples in the Lamaze class. All of them are actual couples with wedding rings. We're all first-time parents, but Allie's the only one who is pregnant with twins. I want to scream that trumps them all, but that would be inappropriate.

"This is a birthing room," Erika, our instructor, says as we walk into a spacious hospital room. It has wallpaper with flowers. There's a bassinet in the corner and a blue couch and a patterned recliner. Pictures of sunsets and sunrises over water are hung around the room. "We have a dimming feature for the lights." Erika lowers the fluorescent lights. "For a more soothing feel while you're laboring."

I gotta admit, it's a nice room.

"But..." Erika touches Allie's arm. "Let's take a look at an operating room since that's where you'll be."

"Oh. Yeah." Allie pretends she's down for that, but I know she'd much rather deliver here.

"We might as well show everyone. I don't want to scare you, but emergencies happen and one of you might end up there as well."

We follow Erika through two doors that say Restricted Access. Another nurses' station is behind the door, with three different openings with beds. Right now, they're all empty.

"So, Allie, you'll be brought back here, and the nurses will monitor both babies until you're ready to go into the operating room. Fisher, so you know, the dads stay here until the mom is ready and on the table." She smiles sweetly, but I tighten my hand on Allie's hip.

"Why's that?" I ask.

Allie bumps me with her hip, but screw that.

"It's just for safety. They'll give her a spinal block to make sure she's numb from the belly down. Once everything is ready, you'll get into scrubs and join her for the birth."

"What if someone forgets to get me?"

Allie hip checks me again.

Erika's crowfeet indent farther. "That's never happened."

"Ever?" I ask, and her eyes narrow. I've upset her.

"No. Never. Now follow me." She pushes through the doors.

"Relax," Allie says in a hushed voice. "I won't push until you're there."

"Push? Won't you have a C-section?" Erika asks, turning in the empty hallway to face Allie.

"I'm hoping to have them vaginally," she says, and Erika's eyes widen in judgment.

"Oh, sweetheart, speaking as someone who had a kid that way, go with the C-section. You can schedule it and"—she leans in—"everything down there stays nice and in place."

"Well, I'm not really concerned about that. I'd rather not have them cut through layers of fat and muscle and have it take months to fully heal. How will I manage to take care of two babies if I can only climb the stairs once a day and can't get on and off the bed easily?"

As far as I've pushed Allie, I've never encountered this side of her. She's snippy, yes, but her voice is direct and powerful and it's clear she won't be easily swayed.

Erika dismisses Allie with a flippant, "Everyone has a birth plan, but be prepared for the unexpected."

When Erica pushes open the doors of an operating room, I feel Allie deflating next to me. It couldn't be more opposite of the calm birthing room we just came from. Everything is gray and sterile and cold looking. I find myself agreeing with Allie—I don't want my babies to come out of the nice warm womb to be assaulted by huge lights shining in their eyes. Talk about traumatic.

"What are those for?" I ask, looking at two long boards on either side of the main table.

"It's where my arms will be secured," Allie whispers.

"Jeez, I hope I have a normal birth!" one of the women in our group says.

Allie turns to give her the death glare.

"Not that... I mean, if I had twins of course..." The woman stops rambling because the pregnant silence in the room says it all. Pun fully intended.

There's a big difference between a vaginal birth and a C-section. I understand why Allie would rather have the babies vaginally now.

Erika files the group out of the operating room, but I tug on Allie's hand to keep her back with me for a second. Placing my hands on her cheeks, I wait for her to look me in the eye. She looks as if she's a minute from losing it.

"It doesn't matter where the babies get delivered, as long as they're healthy. This is something we might not have a choice on, but we'll take them home to a beautiful calming nursery that we'll decorate, and they're going to be just fine."

She nods and a few tears slip down her face, but she inhales to stop her emotions from getting the best of her. She looks around. "It's just so... stark."

"We could always tell my grandma and Dori to decorate it. If anyone could pull it off, it would be them." I grin.

She laughs. "True."

I tighten my hold. "We got this. We're gonna be just fine."

I tug her by the elbows into me until I swallow her in a bear hug. I kiss the top of her head, feeling something shift between us.

Chapter Eighteen

Allie

I return home from the grocery store to find Fisher on the couch with his feet up, reading my *What to Expect When You're Expecting* book. I clear my throat to grab his attention and he glances at me, the book open between his hands.

I never imagined what Fisher would look like if he were an avid reader, but he looks hot. Worn jeans, tight Henley, and barefoot is a good look on him.

"Whatcha reading?" I ask, especially since that book was on my nightstand.

"Sorry. I went into your room to grab your laundry and saw it. I don't want you going up and down the basement stairs anymore. They're steep and if you lose your footing..." He stops talking when he sees my look. The one to suggest he's being overprotective, although he's right. I had quite a scare last week when I thought I was on the bottom step, and I wasn't. I didn't fall, but my stomach felt as if it landed at my feet.

"You are not doing my laundry," I say.

He smirks. "Sorry, it's in the washer already."

"Well, I'll fold because—"

"Don't worry, I'm not a creepo who's smelling your dirty panties." He looks at the book for a moment. "I'm not sure I should read this. It's a lot of information. Information I'm not sure the dad is supposed to know. And how come there's not a book called, *What to Expect When You're Expecting Twins?*"

"There's a chapter on multiples in there." I unzip my new coat from when we went shopping. After placing my purse on the table by the door, I hang my coat up on the hook.

"A chapter? What good is that?" He sounds as offended as I felt when I was searching online for a book on expecting multiples.

"There are some other books about expecting twins," I say, sitting next to him on the couch. "I have groceries in the car," I whisper to get him off his rant.

Ever since our visit to the operating room, he's been very concerned about why everything isn't equal between those having twins and those having a singleton.

He shuts the book and slides to the edge of the couch cushion. "Isn't this, like, the holy grail of pregnancy books?"

I nod, biting my lip to stop from laughing. He's cute when he's like this.

"It says here how much multiple birth rates are up, so why not their own book?" He drops the book on the table, shaking his head. After slipping on his gym shoes, he heads out the front door.

I follow, wishing I could keep my smile tamped down. "I think a lot of the stuff is the same."

He looks at me from over his shoulder. "How? You have two humans inside you, and they have one."

I place my hand on his shoulder. "Let's let this go."

We're supposed to go on a date tonight, but he hasn't mentioned anything since we were in the janitor's closet. I'm wondering if it's still on. I need to know if it's worth the effort of shaving my legs.

"Fine, consider it dropped. It did get me thinking about names though. Should we have names already?"

He's right. There's a high chance I could go to the doctor very soon and have Stella tell me it's time. There are a lot of risks with twins.

"There's no definite time for names. We could name them after they arrive?"

He picks up all the bags of groceries and puts a case of water on his shoulder—a bonus to living with a big strong guy. If I was by myself, I would've left the case of water in the trunk and just taken a bottle as I needed it.

"What do you want to do?" he asks.

I've thought about names, but there's been so much on my mind recently that I pushed it aside. "I'd rather know names before they arrive."

He turns around, almost knocking me over since I'm so close behind him. "Me too!"

I've never heard his voice sound like this—like a kid who just discovered a friend loves the same thing as he does.

"Okay, I guess we'll get some baby name books." I open the back door for him and he walks in.

"We'll stop on the way out of town. I'll message Presley and see if she carries any."

I busy myself opening the bags and taking out the groceries I bought. "So, we are going out tonight?"

He drops the water on the floor with a thud before he puts some in the fridge. "Yeah. I thought that's what we decided? But I wondered if maybe we could go around four this afternoon?"

The clock on the microwave reads two. I have two hours to shave and get ready? "Yeah. I just... where are we going?"

"I want to surprise you, but just dress comfy."

I look down at my jogging pants and sweatshirt. "I'm not sure I could get comfier than this."

He chuckles. "I'll knock on your door at three thirty."

"I thought you said four?"

At the panic in my tone, he looks over his shoulder. "I want to get there by four. Is that a problem?"

"No," I lie. "Do you mind putting these groceries away for me so I can start getting ready?"

He takes the cereal out of my hands. "No problem." With a wink, he turns back to the pantry.

I head to my bedroom, and once I've combed through my closet, I look at the outfit I picked out. A pair of leggings with a big ol' maternity shirt and a cardigan. It's the best I can do with the limited amount of maternity clothes available in Alaska. I could order some online, but I don't want to order clothes that might not fit me.

When I reach the bathroom, I look at my razor, then down at my protruding belly. My toes are still barely in view. I can do this. I sit in the tub and put the water on and psych myself up as if I'm an Olympic athlete going for gold. Then I lean forward and to the side and to the other side. No position is comfortable, and I feel like a Cirque du Soleil performer at this point. I drop the razor. At only six months, I'm too big to shave. That just seals the deal.

There will be no sex tonight.

Maybe the universe is saving me from myself.

FISHER KNOCKS on my bedroom door at three thirty sharp.

I spritz on a squirt of perfume, then open the door.

He's standing in a newer-looking pair of dark jeans and

a sweater, his hair gelled in a way that gives it a just-fucked look. I'll admit one thing, I couldn't have picked a more gorgeous man to procreate with.

"Ready?" he asks and holds out his hand.

On the way down the stairs, a thought occurs to me. "Have you ever even been on a date?"

He chuckles softly, grabbing his keys and wallet. I'm about to take my jacket from the hook when Fisher does it for me and holds it open for me to step into.

"I have. Though not many, I'll admit."

A small part of me feels honored, and another part of me is jealous of those other women. Because although things are progressing and Fisher has been honest about wanting to see where this connection between us can lead, I wonder if I might always second-guess that it's only because I'm the mother of his children.

We make our way to his truck, and he opens the door for me. I step up, using the grab bar to help me, and he shuts the door behind me.

Nothing feels different between us until he parks outside Truth or Dare Brewery.

"Oh, we're going to the brewery?" I ask, trying to keep the disappointment out of my voice.

He turns off the ignition and shakes his head. "I'm not that out of the game."

With no other answer, he gets out, grabbing a backpack out of the back seat, then makes his way over to open my door. Taking my hand, he winds us around the buildings to get into the heart of Sunrise Bay downtown. We walk on the sidewalk and enter The Story Shop, where Presley is wearing a crown and hosting story time for a bunch of kids. When she spots Fisher, she points toward a book on the back of the counter by the cash register.

He grabs the book, then heads back to me. I'm enthralled with the way Presley reads to the little kids. She does different voices and almost acts out each character.

"I think we need to hire her to read bedtime stories," I whisper.

"Good thing she's their aunt."

It's the first time I'm realizing that Presley will be my babies' aunt. And then my mind drifts to the topic of godparents. Will he want one of his brothers and their wives, or will he pick someone and I pick someone? Are they better off with a couple? Of course, I want Stella to be the godmother, but Fisher doesn't know Kingston. How do other couples decide these things?

He nudges his arm to my shoulder and nods for us to leave, so I follow him out the door.

"Have you thought about godparents?" I ask while we walk down toward the Sunbay Inn that's owned by his step-sister, Mandi.

He chuckles. "No."

"I think we have to decide. There's a lot we probably need to figure out. Do we have to get a lawyer involved to figure out custody?"

He stops walking and I don't realize it for a few steps. I circle back around to find him staring at me. "Why would we need a lawyer?"

"We're not married. What if things go south? Maybe this is something we should figure out while we're getting along." Our first date probably wasn't the best time to bring this up, but I probably shouldn't be pregnant with his twins on our first date either.

"I don't wanna talk about it," he says, walking forward and leading the way.

"We'll have to at some point," I say to his back.

I assume we're headed to the restaurant attached to the inn, but Fisher bypasses it to walk along the side toward the beach area.

"Hey," I say, grabbing his coat sleeve to stop him. "I wasn't trying to ruin the evening."

He nods and steps into me. "I'm trying here, and you've already destroyed us in your mind."

He looks over at the inn. I suppose there are some people looking out at us, or rather at the view of the bay.

"I'm just trying to be prepared."

"Let's just enjoy tonight and leave all that for tomorrow, okay?"

He's right. Tonight shouldn't be about godparents and custody of our children. We should enjoy each other's company.

Taking my hand, Fisher guides me onto a walkway past the inn and through a line of trees. There's a hiking trail I never knew about, and we go up a small hill that leaves me breathless, and I have to stop a few times. We walk until we're at the top of the trees on a ledge where I assume people must watch the sunrise over the bay.

"Turn around," he says.

I do as he instructs, and I'm floored by the view of the sunset over the entire town of Sunrise Bay. The sky is filled with purple and pink hues that remind me of a watercolor painting. "Wow, it's gorgeous."

He takes off his backpack and removes a blanket, laying it across the large rock formation. "Don't worry, I'll help you get back up."

He holds out his hand for me to accept and helps me lower to the ground. Then he takes out some cookies and a carton of milk, as well as two champagne flutes.

"Oh my god," I say, completely smitten.

"One day we'll be adults with proper drinks and cheese and crackers, but how about a snack while we watch the sunset?"

It's chilly out, but he holds me close, and I rest my head on his chest. His body heat seeps into me and I warm as though I were sitting next to a crackling fire. We watch the sun move lower in the sky over his hometown. I turn my head toward him as the sky turns burnt orange and tangerine. Nature is really showing off tonight.

"Thanks, Fisher," I whisper.

He tugs on a strand of my hair that's loose from under my hat. "For what?"

"For helping me feel like a woman, not just an incubator."

He inches up on his hands and bends his head toward mine. He's going to kiss me. My lips tingle with anticipation. Maybe it's stupid to pursue this, but don't I owe my children this on some level? To try to be with their father? My ability to resist this man has been worn thinner than a pencil shaving.

He brushes his lips against mine and we breathe each other in for a moment. When his tongue swipes to part my lips, I open. I'll remember this kiss forever.

Then the right side of my breast vibrates from his phone ringing.

He pulls back. "Shit, sorry."

I sit up and he digs out the phone, tugs off his glove, and swipes the screen. "Greene." There's a long pause, then he sighs. "Be right there."

"What is it?" I ask.

"Rylan and his friends just got caught." He takes our empty glasses and cookies, shoving them in the backpack.

I frown. "Caught doing what?"

"Breaking into Chip's house to use the Netflix account."

My eyes widen.

"Fucking teenagers," he mumbles. "We'll have to continue this down at the station."

I suppose this is the life of the sheriff's girlfriend... or wannabe girlfriend, in my case. One day, I'll get that kiss.

Chapter Nineteen

Fisher

"*I*'m sorry about this." I look across the cab of the truck at Allie and cringe.

"It's okay. Family first."

Thank goodness she thinks the same way my entire family does. We have each other's backs and blood is thicker than water. Though Cam isn't my blood, but he's definitely family.

With my lips pressed into a thin line, I dial up my dad on my Bluetooth. "It's weird to be on the other side of this phone call. I'm used to being in Rylan's position."

"What's up, Fisher?" Dad answers.

I cut right to the chase. "Your youngest is at the police station."

"What did he do?" He groans and covers the receiver. "*Marla!*"

"You know the Netflix break-ins?"

Allie looks at me at when we reach a stoplight, teeth pressed into her bottom lip. Lips I almost got to kiss if it weren't for my kid brother.

"You'd better be kidding me."

"Afraid not. I guess the kid takes after his older brothers." It's probably not the best time for me to make a joke, but I hope to lighten the mood.

"Fucking hell," my dad says.

"Oh, and you're on speaker with Allie in the truck." Figure I'll clue him in just in case he gets too carried away.

"What's going on?" Marla says in the background.

"Your damn son is a delinquent," he says.

"What?" Marla's voice grows closer to the receiver. "Who? Jed or Rylan? Who is this? Hello?"

"Hey, Marla, it's Fisher. Rylan got picked up and he's at the station. I'm on my way over now, but Mato says he's pretty sure he and his friends are the Netflix culprits."

"I knew he's been up to no good. So secretive all the time. We'll meet you there. Thanks, Fisher." She hangs up before I can say anything.

"I wouldn't want to be Rylan right now," Allie says.

"I've been Rylan and I'm worried that at fourteen, he might not care."

Silence fills the truck for a minute, and I want to change the subject. Since my goal for tonight was to get to know Allie better, I decide to ask her a question.

"I remember you saying your parents are in Hawaii?"

"Yeah, they moved there a long time ago. Hardly ever return."

"Are you an only child?" I ask, because it's unusual— now that I think about it—that I haven't been introduced to any family members.

"Yep and... well... I'm not very close to my family since my grandparents died." She side-eyes me as though she's worried how I'll feel about that. "It's not that I don't want us to be close. We're just not. I was ready to volunteer to be a part of the Bailey family if they'd have me." A nervous laugh squeaks out of her.

I put my hand on her knee. "Now you're a Greene, so you made out so much better than being a Bailey." I wink at her and run my hand up her thigh, wishing she was wearing a dress and we didn't have somewhere to be.

"I'm not a Greene," she says. "My kids are."

"Maybe you don't have the last name, but you're a Greene now."

She doesn't respond. "Until…"

I squeeze her knee, but we pull into the station before we can dig deeper. "You can hang out in my office while I scare some sense into these kids."

I climb out of the truck. Instead of waiting for me, she opens the door of the truck and exits.

"We're still on our date," I tell her, and she giggles.

"Unless we're just stopping in for handcuffs to use later, I think our date is on a hiatus." She winds her arm through mine. "Which is fine. I loved the sunset." Her cheek lies on my arm and her eyes twinkle with a happiness I don't think I've seen since before our one-night stand.

"You're too awesome." I place my finger under her chin and bend down, placing a gentle kiss on her lips.

"I know." We share a smile before we walk into the station.

Rylan is sitting on the bench out front with his friend Declan and… two girls. I do a double take. Rylan stands, but I hold up my hand to him.

"I'll be back," I say.

Allie is too busy looking over her shoulder to follow me, but she eventually catches up and I walk her into my office.

"That's Calista Bailey," she whispers.

"I know."

"I thought they hated one another?" she continues to whisper.

"They can't hear you," I tell her. My office is in the back of the station.

"Should I call Stella?"

"No. If anything, we'll call her parents. You sit tight. I can grab you something from the vending machine. Want a soda or a snack?"

She sits in the chair behind my desk and twists it around. "This is fun. What must a desk job feel like?" She continues to spin herself around like a five-year-old, but I love seeing her so happy.

"I wouldn't know. I'm barely in that chair."

She stops and runs her hands up and down the arms. "It's a nice chair."

"I'll take your word for it. Okay, I'll be back."

She pulls out the baby name book and searches my drawers until she finds a yellow highlighter. She holds it up like the winning lottery ticket. "Bingo!"

"What are you doing?"

"I'll highlight, then you highlight. We'll compare and match, then go from there."

I freeze, watching her tongue slide out of her mouth as she opens the book, leaning back in my chair and placing her feet up on the edge of my desk. Not about to let this moment go, I pull out my phone and snap a picture.

"What are you doing?" she screeches.

"Remembering you in this moment. The babies will appreciate it when they're older." I make the picture my wallpaper.

"I'm not cool with pictures of me looking like I ate a whale."

"Only a sea lion," I joke, and she narrows her eyes.

"Go handle your business, Sheriff, so you can take me for pizza after."

"Yes, ma'am."

I walk out of my office and shut the door. Mato stops me

in the hall and tells me how a neighbor called while they were breaking into Chip's house. When he showed up, they tried to slip out the window they'd sneaked into the house through, but he nabbed them. He said the girls didn't try to run at all and he had a bit of a foot chase with the boys. I guess chivalry isn't a thing for fourteen-year-olds because the boys left the girls high and dry.

"Does Chip want to press charges?" I ask, crossing my fingers he remembers what it's like to be a boy trying to impress a girl. I do, and I'm already worried about karma coming back to screw me with my own kids.

"He said he's thinking about it." Mato rolls his eyes.

I shake my head. We both know Chip is unlikely to press charges. He once caught a guy red-handed trying to hot-wire his truck in his driveway and gave the guy a pass. I head over to where Rylan glances up from the corner of his eye when he sees me approach.

"The four of you, head to the back." I turn, heading to one of the interrogation rooms. I point at Rylan. "You three in there with Deputy Mato, you with me."

The minute the door shuts, Rylan starts up. "It was just a joke. We never stole anything. Not even a soda."

"You broke into a house that isn't yours." I pull out a chair. "Sit."

"Through unlocked windows. It's not like we actually broke anything."

"It's not your house, Ry. That's the entering part of breaking and entering. It's called trespassing. And why the hell do you have Calista Bailey with you? I thought you hated her."

He stares at his Vans and shrugs.

"Rylan," I say, "this gets worse if you aren't honest."

"Declan likes her," he says softly.

I sit on the edge of the table. "Is this some demented double date? 'Come out with me and we'll break into people's houses to make them think they're crazy'?" He shrugs again and I groan. "One more shrug and I'm throwing you in a damn cell. Out with it."

Finally, he makes eye contact. "I don't know, okay? We saw this guy online who'd do it when he went on vacation. Like if someone didn't sign themselves out of their account, he'd watch all this weird stuff on their account to ruin their recommendations. We thought it was funny." He shrugs.

I can't blame the kid. It's funny as hell. When George Lehmann told me he didn't understand why Netflix would suggest *The Kissing Booth* to him when he only watches documentaries about war and history, I'd had to tamp down my laugh imagining his confusion.

"Then do it to your own damn family. Hell, between you and Calista, you have about twenty houses you could hit. Not to mention the retirement home. If Chip presses charges, you're in serious trouble."

"What about the other houses?" he asks, his voice meek.

"Guess we'll have to see." That's untrue. I have no way to prove they were there but he doesn't need to know that. "Just FYI, your parents are on their way."

His eyes widen, and if I didn't know better, I'd say it looks as if he has tears forming in them. "No! Why couldn't you just handle this? Dad's gonna kill me."

"Ground you, not kill you, and you deserve it," I say.

He nods, frowning.

"I'll be back." I head out of the room to the one with the other three kids, but as I open the door to step in, Allie peeks her head out of my office door. "What are you doing?"

"I'm bored."

"What about the baby names?"

Her nose scrunches. "I don't have it in me. Did you see how big that book is?"

I chuckle. "So what do you want to do?"

"Can I shadow you?" Again, her eyes light up and it makes her that much harder to say no to.

"You can't say anything," I tell her. Usually I'd never allow this, but I know Chip isn't going to press charges, so this is really just me giving kids a scare.

"Yay!" She claps and does a little dance.

I shoot her a look to quiet down and her shoulders sink. She places her finger over her lips.

"Sorry. I'll be good." She salutes me.

With a shake of my head, I walk into the room with the other three kids. "Mato, can you check with Chip to see if he's gonna press charges?"

He looks at Allie, obviously perplexed as to why she's in here.

"Sure." He eyes her as he walks out of the interrogation room.

After the door shuts, I go to introduce Allie. "I'm Sheriff Greene and this is—"

Calista runs to Allie and grabs her hand. "You're my aunt's friend. Please don't tell her. I didn't want to do it."

"Yes, she did!" the other girl says loudly. "She wanted to impress Rylan."

"What?" Declan stands from his seat. "I thought she liked me?"

The other girl leans back in her chair, putting her feet up on the table and chomping on a piece of gum. "Are you blind? Don't you see them together?"

Calista says nothing, but she and Allie share a look.

"FYI, sheriff dude, my dad's a lawyer, so I'd like to use my phone call now," Declan says.

Allie hugs Calista and looks at me over her head, clearly questioning what I'm going to do.

"First of all, you're not arrested… yet. And you're under-age, so your dad will be called to come and get you."

Declan slouches in his chair. "Screw Rylan, all the girls like him."

"I don't understand why," the other girl remarks, inspecting her nails.

I've got one kid scared shitless in the room next door, Calista Bailey in tears, Declan is heartbroken, but this other girl couldn't give a shit. What is wrong with today's youth?

I put a scare into the kids before I call their parents. I know how hard it can be to live in a small town when you're a teen and feel like nothing fun is ever going on. Sometimes boredom leads to trouble—idle hands and all that. This is their one get-out-of-jail-free card, but if I see any of them in my station again, there will be no free pass.

Dad and Marla show up, and Mato stands to let them in. I nod to Dad to go ahead and talk to Rylan.

Calista watches the exchange of my dad and Marla lecturing Rylan down the hallway, and she turns to me. "Do you think he's in a lot of trouble?" Her concern for him is surprising.

An hour later, all the parents have come to pick up their kids and it's just Allie, Mato, and me left in the office.

"You ready?" I ask Allie.

"For bed."

Mato's eyes widen and he pretends to be looking over paperwork, but I think it's just the menu from Two Brothers and an Egg.

"I meant to sleep," Allie clarifies. "Not to sleep—"

"You don't have to explain yourself to Mato." I laugh, and Allie groans.

"No worries, I'd rather not hear all the details about Fisher in bed."

"That's not what I meant," she argues.

I put my arm around her shoulders. "Let's go."

"See you two tomorrow," Mato says. "I guess I don't have to bother lecturing you two on practicing safe sex."

I flip him off as we walk out of the office.

This date didn't exactly go how I'd planned, but I had a great time because of the woman I was with.

Chapter Twenty

Allie

I'm eating lunch in the cafeteria when a heavy perfume accosts my nostrils. I look up from my book to see Dori and Ethel one table away and coming toward me. I quickly shut my book and shove it in my bag.

"Ladies," I say. I hope they're not here to try to get intel from me about what happened with Rylan and Calista at the police station because I'm pleading the Fifth. Last I heard, they'd both been grounded for the foreseeable future and didn't have access to any electronics—including Netflix.

They both take a seat and share a look as though they're about to divulge juicy gossip.

"It's okay if you're reading one of those spicy romance novels. Midge keeps some in her bottom drawer," Dori says.

"Why in her bottom drawer?" I ask.

Ethel pats my hand as if maybe I'm losing it. "Because she wants to hide it."

"Midge?" I'm surprised that woman would care. I mean, from what I've heard, she's slept with a lot of the men at Northern Lights. So what if she reads romance novels? I shake my head at the absurdity. "It's a book about pregnancy. What are you two doing here?"

"We're old, sweetie, we always know someone in the hospital," Dori says.

"It's either here or the funeral home," Ethel adds.

I guess they have a point, but unease makes my stomach clench at the thought of getting older and knowing my years are limited. Although these two still live their lives to the fullest.

I push out my chair. "I have to get back to work. It was nice seeing you."

"How are things with you and Fisher?" Dori asks before I can stand. "I mean, you two are in an unusual situation… we just want to make sure you're doing well."

"Speaking of, how is my apartment coming along?"

She sits back in her seat and fidgets with her hands. "You know how contractors are. So slow." She shrugs.

"But you're Dori Bailey. I wouldn't think you'd take that from them?" I ask, seeing she's becoming flustered.

"I'm not that intimidating."

"Hmm…" I pick up my tray and grab my bag, swinging it over my shoulder, then stand. "Have a great day, ladies."

They're quick to follow, which I only know from the scent of their flowery perfume.

I put my tray away and turn back around. "What's really going on?"

Dori nudges Ethel and she looks at her in panic, so Dori nods toward me.

I rest my hands on my belly. "Just spit it out, ladies."

"I wanted to invite you and Fisher over. I have some heirlooms I'd like to give you for the babies."

"Okay," I say.

"Really?" Ethel's eyes light up.

"Yep."

She stares at my stomach. "May I?" Hands with age spots and paper-thin skin are outstretched toward me.

I smile. "Go ahead."

"Thank you. First Noah and Emilia and now these little ones. I feel so honored to be this blessed." She looks up at me, her eyes twinkling with happiness, and warmth spreads across my chest.

I listen to Ethel and Dori talk about the joy a baby brings to a family and become even more excited for them to be born. I try to picture the babies. Between Fisher and me, they'll likely have dark hair and dark eyes with olive complexions. Such a stark contrast to baby Noah.

"I have to get to work. When do you want us to come by? Have you talked to Fisher?"

"You guys coordinate your schedules and let us know." Ethel runs her hand over my belly one more time and steps back.

"Great. I'll be in touch."

I say goodbye to both women, unsure what they could be planning but knowing they're definitely planning something. There was too much hesitation on Ethel's part to ask me to come over. Heirlooms? Sure, whatever.

Before I head back to the emergency room, I send Fisher a quick text about going to his grandma's, to which I get a reply that's simply a line of question marks. Dori and Ethel are going to have to up their game if they want to get one over on the two of us.

FISHER and I decide to get the visit to Northern Lights over with. Whatever they're trying to accomplish won't change whether we go now or a month from now.

Walking into Northern Lights, we're stopped by a woman wearing a LeeAnn nametag. "Sorry, guys, we just had a situation. Give me a minute."

"Is Grandma in her apartment?" Fisher asks.

"No, we just finished dinner service. I don't think your grandma is in her suite. Let me grab her for you."

We stand off to the side next to a fake plant.

"You don't think they're planning a baby shower, do you?" I ask.

Fisher looks at me. "I wouldn't put anything past them. Speaking of, don't we need a baby shower? And to register for some stuff? I remember having to go to the store when Nikki was pregnant, and she told them what she wanted."

I laugh because this daddy version of Fisher is too cute. "Yeah. I've been checking out different stuff, but I haven't registered or anything yet. I'm not even sure about a shower."

He chuckles and shakes his head. "Do you really think Marla won't give you a baby shower? Never gonna happen."

No one has said anything to me, and let's be honest, we are in a bit of a weird circumstance. Fisher and I aren't in a romantic relationship. He got me pregnant during a one-night stand. Maybe it would be awkward for his family to throw a baby shower given the circumstances. I know my parents weren't exactly thrilled when I called them to explain the situation. "No one has to do anything for me."

He turns me toward him, and as always, his large palm cradles my cheek. It's my favorite when he does that. "Us. For *us*. And I bought Nikki some overpriced fancy-ass stroller, so she's buying us something."

He bends down and kisses my forehead. Although things are going well with us, we still haven't really made out or slept together. The most we've done is cuddle while watching a movie, but that might be because he's always trying to make sure I'm comfortable.

Ethel comes around the corner with LeeAnn not far

behind, who goes to sit at her desk. "Hey! LeeAnn, why didn't you tell me they were here?"

"Hi, Grandma," Fisher says, his hands dropping from me to give her a hug.

"Hi, Fisher. Hi, Allie." She hugs her grandson and squeezes my hand in greeting. "LeeAnn, this is perfect after what just happened. You have a nurse here and a sheriff."

LeeAnn rolls her eyes. "It's all under control."

"Can I help with something?" I ask.

"Olive just choked on a piece of meat. She's good now," LeeAnn says.

"What if it happens again and none of you are around?" Ethel says.

Dori comes into the lobby to join us. "Ethel's right. You leave us alone all the time. If they teach us what to do, then maybe we can help save one of our own lives."

Fisher side-eyes me, wondering what the hell they're talking about.

"We have plenty of people on staff trained to administer first aid. One of you just has to press the red emergency button and we'll be there." LeeAnn buries her head in the papers at her desk. She sits down, looking annoyed. "But now I have to write up a report so it's in Olive's file."

"You can teach us CPR and the Heimlich." Dori puts her hand in mine, tugging me forward.

"I'm not so sure..."

"Dori and Ethel, please stop." LeeAnn never looks up from her desk.

"They can at least show us what to do." Dori tugs me again.

Fisher blows out a long breath. "I thought we were here for some heirlooms?"

"Yeah, yeah. But we'll just do this really fast. Come on,

LeeAnn." Ethel goes over to the desk and Dori follows her. They all whisper.

LeeAnn looks at us, clearly allowing the two women to swindle her into doing something she doesn't want to.

"I don't want to be responsible for teaching them the Heimlich," I whisper to Fisher.

"Me either. I mean we could break one of their ribs."

I lean in closer. "I say we only display it on each other. We don't use any of them."

He glances at my stomach. "I can't give you the Heimlich and I doubt you can give it to me."

Ugh, he's right.

"Ethel!" I raise my hand. "I'm not sure we can teach you. There's no way with my belly that I can get around Fisher, and he obviously can't practice on me."

She waves me off, continuing to push LeeAnn. A minute later, Fisher groans when we witness LeeAnn nod.

"Who the hell knows what we're gonna be doing now," he mumbles.

"Let's go, you two." Dori waves for us to follow her.

We end up in the cafeteria, but all the food has been cleaned up, tables pushed aside by the workers. I think Dori and Ethel could run the world the way they get people to do things—except fix my apartment, of course.

"I don't even have any of my stuff," I say to Ethel.

"It's okay. Fisher, lie down." She pats the table.

"No."

"Why not?"

"Because this is ridiculous. I'm here for some family heirlooms, not to teach your friends CPR and the Heimlich maneuver." He crosses his arms.

"I'm your grandmother. Your elder." Ethel uses a look I've never seen before, and for a moment, I see a glimpse of what kind of mother she was. Obviously one who never took any shit.

For a moment, I think it might be easier if we go along with this.

"Fine," he grumbles, clearly seeing that too, and gets up on the table.

"What's going on? My show is on!" a man screams from where he's seated.

"Can it, Earl. Ethel's grandson Fisher is the sheriff for Sunrise Bay and his... Allie is a nurse. They're going to teach us how to do CPR in case something happens to one of us."

"About time. You know they don't care about us." A man with a cane raises it.

The staff are all huddled together, rolling their eyes.

Midge raises her hand. "Can I volunteer?"

"No, Midge. You'll probably stick your tongue in Fisher's mouth," Dori says.

Fisher's eyes bulge and he goes to sit up. "I'm out."

"Relax." Ethel pushes him back down. "Only Allie's tongue will be in your mouth—if you're lucky."

I feel my cheeks heat. Fisher's hand reaches for mine and he links our fingers. When I look at him, he mouths that he's sorry and I shake my head. It's okay. Family is family. And I know exactly what these two are like.

"How are we supposed to know if we don't practice ourselves?" Earl asks.

Dori and Ethel look at one another. They can't argue that it's a good point.

"You guys can practice afterward," Ethel says and waves him off.

"I can stop by with some brochures if you'd like." I make the offer so I don't have to witness all these people trying to give CPR to one another.

"Perfect. We'll watch Allie and Fisher, then she'll drop off materials for us." Ethel takes a seat and Dori sits next to her. "Go ahead, guys."

I stand there frozen as if I'm a Broadway actress doing a live show and I've forgotten my lines. "What do you want me to do exactly?"

"Since you can't do the Heimlich, just show us CPR." Dori waves for me to get started.

"But didn't Olive choke?"

"Stop asking questions, just do it. It's almost bedtime," the guy with the cane screams.

"Yeah, and Midge said she's tucking me in," Earl yells. "I'm getting sleepy."

"Let's just get this over with," Fisher whispers.

I step up to the table and I explain how to tilt the head back, pinch the bridge of the nose, and put your mouth over the other person's.

"Do we blow air in?" a woman near the back asks. "Can you demonstrate?"

I ignore her and instead show them how to entwine my hands together to get the heel of my palm to press where the heart is.

"Hello? I don't understand the breathing thing?" the woman says again.

"I could just watch this on that stupid Lifetime channel they have here. I thought you were going to show us the good stuff!" The guy with the cane won't shut up and I'm growing irritated.

"I think she has pregnancy brain," another man says.

"Okay, that's it!" Fisher sits up and looks at them. "Be nice. Neither one of us even—"

I hit him in the back where no one can see. I don't want these people to think we don't want to be here. Who knows how often their loved ones come to visit? For a lot of them, we could be their sole interaction from the outside world.

"It's fine. Okay. I'll show you as best I can, but maybe we need to schedule a class with dummies next time." I send a look at Ethel and Dori and they both look away as though they don't see me.

Fisher lies back down with a sullen look on his handsome face.

"Tip the head like this, then pinch the bridge of their nose." I demonstrate on Fisher. "You want to make sure their airway is unobstructed like this." I gesture with my hand. "And then you're going to open up your mouth wide over theirs, creating a seal of sorts." I lean down. "Ready?"

"As ever." He smiles.

I place my mouth over Fisher's for a millisecond. "Then you'd do the chest compressions." I put my hands together again and place them on Fisher's chest.

"No. No. No. I need to see the mouth thing again. How are you breathing in? One long breath, a bunch of short ones?" The woman with curlers in her hair continues to be a pain in the ass.

Fisher looks at his grandma. "Is this what you want?"

He swings his legs to the side, places his hand on the back of my head, and smashes our lips together.

At first my eyes are wide open in surprise, but he swipes his tongue along my lips to part them and I open for him. God, I forgot how great of a kisser he is. I melt into his body and step between his legs. His short beard is rough against my skin and makes it tingle. The world tilts and stars fill my vision as my pulse pounds between my legs. I fist his shirt, not wanting to let him go.

Cheers and whistles commence, making Fisher close the kiss. He jumps off the table.

"There. Now we're going to go." He takes my hand and leads me toward the exit of the cafeteria.

"Now I'm horny," Midge says.

"Come on down to my room," a man says.

"Thank you all for helping us out," Dori says.

I shake my head, looking over my shoulder at Ethel, who winks at me before Fisher drags me through the sliding doors. They're seriously evil, but the fact that Fisher won't play their little game makes me fall for him a little more.

The question is, did he kiss me only to get them to shut up or because he wanted to? It's startling how much I hope it's the latter. Startling and maybe a little concerning.

Fisher

"You're actually trusting me with this?" Chevelle asks as we look around the store.

It specializes in lotions, bath stuff, and candles.

"I'm getting nauseous from all the smells in here," Cam says, picking up another bottle of lotion and testing it on his skin.

"Stop putting them on," Chevelle tells him, sounding exasperated.

"I can't stop. It's addicting." Cam strolls through, stopping to try another fragrance.

"So?" Chevelle asks, ignoring Cam.

"I'm out of my league, okay? But I really want to..." I'm not a "heart on my sleeve" kind of guy, but I want to pamper Allie.

"So... do you like her?" my sister asks, grinning.

I pick up a candle that's supposed to smell like vanilla and tobacco. Interesting. "Of course I like her."

Cam leans in. "But do you *like* like her?"

Chevelle laughs, and I don't like the look they share.

"What are we, in the first grade?"

Chevelle continues putting things in the basket hanging

from her arm. "You know what he means. You've never gone to this much effort for anyone before."

I dodge them, turning the other way because I'm confused. I keep trying to convince myself that I'm not a commitment guy, but the more I'm with Allie, the more I want her for myself. The thought of her meeting someone else, of someone else seeing her different smiles, is like a knife in the gut. But I can't lay my heart on the line unless I'm absolutely sure. Giving her false hope will only leave her disappointed and hurt, and I can't do that to the mother of my children.

"You *like* like her, don't you?" Cam whispers, checking to make sure Chevelle isn't around. I push him and he laughs. "I fucking knew it. I'm not sure why you're denying it."

"I'm not denying it. It's just no one's business."

Chevelle walks over and joins us. "I think Mom would have liked Allie. She's caring and sweet and deals with your bullshit."

Chevelle doesn't talk about Mom all that often. None of us really do. I think besides my mom's birthday celebration every year and the anniversary of her death, we all keep those memories bottled up. I know if I told Chevelle I opened up to Allie about Mom, she'd tell me I'm an idiot because that means I've definitely fallen for Allie. And she'd be right. But for some reason, I'm still worried it's lust and not love.

"Okay, so you have candles, lotions, oils, face masks, and scrubs in here. I included a foot and nail kit because I'm sure she can't do it herself anymore. I can't even imagine what she's going through. Does she shave?" Chevelle asks. "I remember Nikki was getting waxed regularly."

I shrug and look at Cam, but thankfully he's over at the air freshener area. He sneezes after bringing a sample to his nose and inhaling it as if it's cocaine. God, why did I drag him here with me?

"These are things you need to find out." Chevelle pokes me in the stomach. "I think it's great, you know. The fact that you're moving on from your bachelor phase—even if it took you an unplanned pregnancy to do it. The best thing that might've happened is that condom breaking." She pokes me again and passes me the basket. "Oh, and I put a bottle of bubble bath in there for me as payment." She smiles brightly and walks away.

I head to the register and try not to be shell-shocked when the cashier tells me the total. Allie's worth it and more. But Jesus, women get hosed with the price of this shit.

"Fisher's gonna get laid," Cam says as we're leaving the store.

"What are you, thirteen?" Chevelle rolls her eyes. "Grow up, Cam."

"It was a joke, okay? I'm not salivating for him to give me specifics of what her tits feel like or anything."

Chevelle doesn't bother acknowledging his response. "I'm starved. Lunch, fellas?"

"I gotta finalize some things at the station before heading home to surprise her."

"I'm game," Cam says, a little too eagerly for my liking, and I wonder if I should change my mind and join them.

"See you." Chevelle kisses my cheek. "She's just as lucky as you," she whispers in my ear. "You deserve happiness, Fisher."

I nod. "Thanks for your help."

"What about me?" Cam asks, shaking my hand.

We share a man hug, and I give him a look I hope he interprets as "stay the hell away from my little sister."

"Gross, Cam. You smell like you've been with about ten different woman at once." She shakes her head.

"Who says it hasn't happened before?" He grins, and Chevelle swats him across the upper arm.

They leave, climbing into Cam's truck, and I wait for them to drive off before I get into my own truck. I lied when I said I had to stop by the station. I'm not sure how long this is going to take to set up and I want it to be perfect, just like Allie.

THERE's hot water in the bathtub, pink rose petals floating from end to end. Lines of candles are lit on the bathroom counter and around the tub.

"Hey, Allie!" I call to her.

"What's up?"

"Just come up here," I call from her bathroom.

She's been obsessed with a show on Netflix about three suburban women who launder money, but I'm hopeful she'll be cool with putting that on pause to come up here. I hear her footsteps on the stairs. I told her I was taking a shower so she wouldn't suspect anything when she heard the water running.

"Fisher, why are you in my room again?" At least I hear what I think is amusement in her voice.

"Technically it's my room…"

My words fade as she stands in the doorway, a smile creeping up on her face. It's my favorite smile, the one when she's happy because I did a nice thing for her.

"What is this?" She steps in and her smile deepens. "Fisher?"

"A bath, and afterward a massage?" I feel way more sheepish and unsure than I've ever been with a woman.

She sits on the edge of the tub and dips her hand in. She retracts it quickly. "It's going to feel heavenly."

"Not too hot," I say. "I was afraid because of the babies."

She laughs and stands, placing her dry hand on my chest. "The babies will be fine. You did the temperature perfect." Inching up on her toes, she places a sweet kiss on my lips. "How about you join me?"

My eyes widen and my dick twitches as my hands fall to her hips. "Seriously? That wasn't my reason for doing this. I just wanted to pamper you a little since you're doing all the heavy lifting with our babies."

She smiles and places my hands on the hem of her sweatshirt. "I'm positive."

I haven't been nervous around a woman since puberty, but my heart is galloping like a runaway horse right now. There's so much we have to talk about and so much I want to tell her.

I slowly raise her sweatshirt up and over her head, finding a T-shirt underneath. I groan. "How many layers are you wearing, woman?"

"Find out," she whispers.

My fingers graze down her sides, picking up the hem of her T-shirt. I pull it up and drop it on the floor, then stare at her in her bra.

"I'm sorry it's not sexier." Her bra is white without a stitch of lace or satin on it. It props up her swollen breasts like they want some attention.

"It's the same result either way." I reach behind her and unclasp the bra, letting the straps fall down her arms. "You're beautiful either way."

She watches me with intent, and with the soft music

playing that was supposed to soothe her, I'm reminded how romantic this scene is now that I'm undressing her.

Her breasts bounce free and all I want to do is touch them. Play with her nipples and see how hard I can get them. But first I need to deal with her pants before the water gets too cold.

I hook my fingers in the elastic waist of her maternity pants and I'm about to drag them down her legs when her hands lock on my wrists.

"Stop!"

I remove my hands, holding them up. "Sorry. Too far? I can wait outside."

She shakes her head. "Fisher." Her head falls to my chest, and I wrap my arms around her.

"What is it?"

"I haven't shaved. I tried the other day and I'm just too big. I got a cramp in my side."

I chuckle lightly and place my hands on her upper arms, stepping back so she has no choice but to look up at me. Once we're parted enough, I grasp her chin and lift her face to look at me. "I don't care."

"But I do." There's a whine to her tone.

I'm not sure I can convince her to change her mind. Hair on her legs isn't going to stop my quest to have her.

"We've only been together once. And now the second time, I'm huge and have a hairy pussy and legs." She sits on the edge of the tub, frowning.

"I'll be right back."

I head out of the room and into the main bathroom I've been using, then return with my razor and shaving cream.

She raises her eyebrows at me. "What are you doing?"

"I'm going to shave you." Her continued cocked eyebrows make me chuckle. "I shave this beautiful face...

well… I did for years. Not so much anymore." I run my hand down my more than five o'clock shadow. "Surely I can handle your legs."

Her head falls into her hands. "This is so embarrassing."

"Come on. It's just me."

She turns to me, and I can see that there's a lot going on in her head. "Have you ever thought how fast this relationship is going? It's like there's no turning back. There's no dating that spreads to weeks or months of seeing each other. There's no sweet good-night kisses followed by a make-out session that leads to groping to sex. It's like we're on warp speed. And we're doing it all backward."

I put my arm around her bare shoulders. "We're just playing the cards we're dealt, and truthfully, I'm not sure that other way would've worked for me."

"What do you mean?" Her forehead wrinkles.

I'm tentative about telling her what's been on my mind. I don't want her doubting that I want to date her. That I'm slowly falling in love with her and not just because she's the mother of my children. But I need to be absolutely sure before I confess to her.

"I'm invested because we're moving fast. Because our children are going to be here soon, and I want us to be in a good place. Because there can't be any second-guessing, I'm going strictly on my gut."

"And?"

"Nothing. I think that if you hadn't been pregnant and we'd gone on a date, I would've second-guessed every decision and we might never get to the part where I'm shaving your legs because I would've run scared or pushed you away. But because of the situation we're in, I was forced to react. And I'm glad, because otherwise I'd be missing out." I bend to kiss her temple. I want to say more, tell her I'm falling in love with her, but I need to be really sure. "Now undress and sink into that water. I'm going to get down to my boxers, shave your legs, then I'm joining you."

"Ugh... okay. I need them shaved and it's either you or Stella. She'd probably tell me no and tell me how many hairy legs and bushes she sees when she delivers babies. I don't need the visual." She stands and hooks her fingers on her pants.

I watch as she shimmies out of them. I never thought I would be here. Not once did I think I would be shaving a woman's legs while she's pregnant with my babies. But here I am.

Long gone are the days of her cute landing strip like when we slept together, but that's okay. I really don't care. I hold out my hand and help her step into the water.

"Oh, it feels so nice." She leans back and closes her eyes.

I stand to unclothe, and she tries to act as though she's not watching, but I know she is. She'll have a visual as I sit on the edge of the tub. I fill a cup with water to clean off the razor so we're not bathing in little hairs.

"Okay, woman, give me your leg." I tap my thigh.

She lifts it and I run water over her leg. They aren't even that bad.

"This is good, right? Am I doing a good job of wooing you?"

Her head falls back in laughter before looking me in the eye. "You're doing great."

That look on her face is enough to convince me that maybe I was wrong, maybe I can do this whole relationship thing, because I'll be damned if some other bastard gets this woman. She's mine.

Chapter Twenty-two

Allie

I watch Fisher fill his palm with shaving cream, and he runs it up the part of my leg that's peeking out from the water. He wets the razor in the cup he filled and winks at me. "Ready?"

"Again..."

"Stop protesting. I'm doing this." He runs the razor up my leg, stopping right before my knee.

He peeks up at me every once in a while to make sure I'm okay. I can only admire his gentleness and think of how it will be passed along to our children once they're born. The way he holds my leg and doesn't put too much pressure on the razor... it's oddly erotic.

"Tell me about your tattoos?" I ask, hoping it distracts me from the growing buzz between my legs.

He glances at his arms and laughs. "Pick one."

There's an array of different tattoos all over his skin. Some are words, a lot are roses, and symbols that I have no idea what they mean. But there's one I've always wondered about, so I decide to ask him about that one.

"Love, Pain, Hate?"

The smile falls from his lips, and he concentrates harder on the razor. "In my experience, love leads to hate because of the pain."

"Your mom?"

He frowns and nods. "But now…"

"What? Tell me."

"I'm starting to realize that by closing myself off, I'm missing out on a lot." He peeks through his dark lashes to check my reaction.

"Is that because of the babies?" I ask, cupping warm water over my protruding belly.

He finishes one leg and sets it gently in the water. I shift to the other end of the tub so my opposite leg is now closest to him, and he starts with the other one. After lathering up the shaving cream, he spreads it across my leg.

"Partly. Like I said, I can't control the love I already have for them. I never thought I'd be put in this situation." He shrugs. "But it's not only the babies, Allie. It's you too."

A flutter unravels in my stomach as if someone has pulled a bow loose.

He chuckles, and I wonder what my facial expression looks like right now. "It's not just because you're carrying our babies." He runs the razor up my leg. "I can't stop thinking about you when you're not around, and when you are here, I can't get enough time with you. I'm not stupid. I know what it means, and I'm exhausted from trying to fight it."

"Fight what?" I ask softly.

"Whatever this is between us."

I'm shocked. Yeah, things have developed between us, but I didn't expect Fisher to be so open and honest with his feelings. I hate that a small part of me still doubts they could be genuine and that they have nothing to do with the babies. I know he said it's not just about the babies, but I desperately want to know if things would be different if I wasn't pregnant. Would we have run into each other again and had sparks fly had we not found ourselves having children together? But for just tonight, I don't want to think about that.

"You feel it, right?" He finishes my second leg much faster than my first, then he puts the razor in the cup and lowers it to the bathroom floor.

I never thought I'd see the day where Fisher Greene looks embarrassed. I think because he's unsure how I feel.

"I'd like nothing more than for us to be together, Fisher. I do feel whatever this is between us, but..." I let the but die on my lips. Mostly because tonight, I want him. I've been denying my feelings for him this entire time because I don't want to get hurt, but it's too late. Whether this ends tonight or in three years, the hurt will come with a vengeance. I might as well come too.

He stands, takes off his boxers, and all I can see is his hardening cock springing north as he sinks into the water opposite me and places my legs on each side of his hips. "Don't stop. Tell me what you were going to say."

I shake my head, loving the sensation of his hands running up and down my now smooth legs. I decide to change the subject. "You do a great job of shaving."

He shoots me a cocky smile and winks. "If you trust me, I bet I can shave your pussy too." Then his smile drops, and he raises his hands. "Not that I care whether it's shaved or not."

I giggle and carefully raise onto my knees, using my hands on either side of the tub to brace myself. Leaning forward, I'm acutely aware of my tits dipping into the water along with my stomach. My belly is a barrier between us, but I'm done holding back.

"Kiss me, Fisher," I tell him in a low voice.

His hand slides out of the water and winds around my

neck, pulling me down toward him, eyes darkening with hunger. "God, Allie, I want nothing more."

His lips are on mine and his tongue immediately seeks entry. I part my lips, and all the tension of whether or not I should cross this line untangles when he draws me closer. I clench inside and ache while his fingers trail down my spine.

His mouth falls from mine and lingers on my neck, casting small kisses. "I want you so fucking bad."

My hand dips below the water, and I hold steady with my other hand on the edge of the tub. I wrap my hand around his silken cock, sliding my palm up and down his hard length. His groans spur me to continue, to tighten my hold and twist when I reach the tip.

"Come here." He situates me so I'm straddling him, and although my belly is in the way, I sit on his thighs so I can continue to pump his cock.

His hands caress and roam, exploring every inch of my body as though he's reveling in what he's been wanting to do for a while. He plucks at my nipples and lifts the weight of my heavy breasts in his hands.

With his hands on my ass, he thrusts me forward, allowing my pussy to be pressed to his dick and holy shit, I close my eyes from the sensation that radiates from my center. I've been so horny this past month, nothing satisfying me the way I need. My moan echoes in the small bathroom while I unapologetically grind along his length, searching for the friction along my clit to make me explode.

"Oh, god," I gasp, my arms wrapping around his neck as leverage.

He allows me to do as I please, helping me with his hands molded to my ass, pushing me against him and lifting slightly. His whiskey eyes are drunk with lust and his mouth draws in short gasps of air.

Sensation overrides any thinking on my part, and I lift slightly to run the tip of his dick along my clit. There's no stopping the inevitable. My orgasm is brimming, and Fisher isn't slowing down. He leans forward and his tongue darts out to my nipple. My body shudders while my pussy clenches.

Wave after wave of ecstasy rolls over me. I don't remember the last time I had such an intense orgasm. Well, I do. The night I conceived these babies.

"You're beautiful when you come. You know that?" His deep voice draws me back to the present.

His dark eyes are intoxicating in the candlelight. My breath catches in my throat from the desire that flares once again.

"I need you out of this water," he says, his lips trailing down my shoulder. "I need to be deep inside you."

Nothing has ever sounded so good. Not even a muffin from Two Brothers and an Egg.

He slides me back and steps out first, grabbing a towel and holding it out for me.

"I thought I was getting a massage," I say, smiling at him and accepting his hand to help me step out.

"We have all night."

He wraps the soft cotton towel around me and rests his hands on my stomach that's still peeking out. I've craved this feeling of safety since I found out I was pregnant and even more so after I found out I was having twins. I've never felt more alone than I did when I looked at the pee stick that told me my entire life was about to change. I remembered Fisher's words, that he wasn't a marriage and kids type of guy. After my phone call went unanswered, I convinced myself that it was all on me, but ever since I moved into Fisher's house, I've come to crave and find comfort in the feeling of doing this with someone else.

He leads me to the bedroom until we're standing at the edge of the bed. Methodically, he weaves the towel around my body, drying me off inch by inch. My eyes follow his movements, and every second or so, he looks up to make sure I'm okay. A woman could get used to this kind of treatment.

After he finishes drying me, he uses the towel on himself, then drops the towel between the two of us, grabs my cheeks, and tilts my head up to his. His lips fall to mine. This time, there's more hunger and intensity, as though maybe he was holding himself back before.

I rise onto my tiptoes, clinging to his biceps, not wanting to ever forget this moment. He turns us around and he crawls up the bed, digging into his nightstand drawer and pulling out some K-Y jelly before he leans back against the headboard. I step to the side of the bed and head toward him.

He squeezes a small amount on two of his fingers and dips them between my legs. "Water dries you out and I don't want to hurt you."

I place a knee on the bed and straddle him again. His fingers run through my folds and his thumb presses small circles on my clit, making me gasp. Then he squirts more and runs it over his dick, holding the base. The vision has me licking my lips and wondering if this is what he looks like when he satisfies himself.

I lift my leg over him, and he guides himself to my entrance. I slowly sink down on his cock and my eyes drift closed as I feel him fill me. He groans and his hands go to my hips, his fingertips pressing into my skin.

"Damn," he says.

I wait a minute, wanting to adjust to his size. He raises his hands to my tits, playing with my nipples like he remembers from his one night with me how much I enjoy that. When I bend forward to kiss him, he pinches my nipples and I groan into his open mouth.

Needing to move, I rise up and slide back and forth. He shifts his hips up off the bed, driving his dick into me. It doesn't take long for us to move faster, for him to thrust harder, our mouths colliding in a frenzy. The longer we go, the more intense we become. Inaudible words are whispered between us, my fingers gripping his tattooed skin, trying to anchor myself to him.

I hate the restriction of my belly, but Fisher doesn't seem to notice nor care. He guides me up and down on his steel length, his fingers digging into my hips, then up my spine, pushing me flush against him.

He cups my breasts and pushes them up, his thumbs brushing my hard nipples. "I've wanted my hands on your tits since that day I saw you naked."

I stare down at him, and he tilts his head, little beads of sweat forming along his hairline. He licks his lips, and my mouth descends on his, my climax accelerating, arousal racing through my body. I know it's coming, and as hard as I clench to try to stop it, I know there's no stopping it. Fisher lifts his hips and drives into me so hard, I gasp his name, my body tensing from the explosion of bliss radiating through my body.

The orgasm hits me hard and fast until I sink down on him again, my limbs relaxing. He grabs my hips and lifts me a bit so he can thrust into me from below. It's the passion filling his eyes that transfixes me as his lips twist and he curses under his breath. His fingertips dig into my flesh as he stills inside me.

"Fuck," he says, and he finishes inside me.

I let myself collapse on his chest and he holds me, goose bumps following the stroke of his fingers up and down my spine.

As he holds me, I'm reminded of why I was worried about this moment in the first place. Fisher might not know it, but I do. I've fallen head over heels in love with this man.

Chapter Twenty-three

Fisher

Now that I've slept with Allie, I'm happy to discover that she's a nympho. I have no idea if it's the pregnancy hormones or just how she feels about me though. My arrogant self wants to think it's me, but I have no complaints either way. She's been rubbing up on me for the past week. We've kept the fact that we're together a secret, not wanting the pressure of other people's expectations weighing on us.

At this moment, I see the benefit of having a girlfriend because the sex is out of this world. It only gets better every time as we get to know each other's bodies and what the other person likes. And it's so different when there are feelings involved and it's just not about getting off.

Of course, truth be told, I knew it would be like this with Allie back in the summer. I just didn't want to admit it to myself.

"I'm nervous she might flip out," I say to Mato, who's walking beside me into the emergency room.

I'm holding a white T-shirt against the cut on my head that I got in an altercation. The guy was drugged out of his mind, and that's always unpredictable. I was trying to talk him down, but he attacked me before I wrestled him to the ground. Luckily Mato came by to check on the situation. After we took the guy back to the station to have Peterson handle him, Mato demanded I get the cut looked at.

"It's a bad gash. You need stitches," he says.

Fran is at the desk, and she stands when I walk in. "Fisher!"

"I'm fine, just maybe some stitches. Allie here?" I ask.

Fran picks up the phone, says she needs help, and rounds the desk, opening the doors to the back.

"I'm fine. I have no idea why you're all making such a big deal." As soon as the words leave my lips, a woozy feeling comes over me and the room spins. I drift over to the wall to steady myself while Mato grips my belt.

"Fisher!" Allie shouts.

A few other people help me into a room and lay me down.

Allie rushes to my side. "What happened?"

"He got cut. It's a bad one, but I didn't think he'd lost that much blood," Mato tells her.

Allie pulls away the white now soaked in blood T-shirt and curses. "It's deep. Head wounds always bleed a lot."

"Fool thought a Band-Aid would fix it," Mato says.

"Of course my tough guy thought that." She touches my ankle, then heads over to the cabinets and pulls supplies from inside.

I like the sound of her calling me her tough guy. "It's not a huge deal." I move to sit up.

"Fisher, if you sit up, I'm going to strap you down," Allie says, pointing at me before turning back to what she's doing.

"Promise?"

Mato laughs. "I'm thinking he's in good hands with you." He clasps my shoulder. "I'll take care of everything with the arrest. You get yourself taken care of." He stops at Allie's side. "Good luck with him. Make sure he keeps his hands to himself." He chuckles and walks out.

Allie comes over, placing the stuff on the table. I try to take her hand, but she's just out of reach.

"Why didn't I get a kiss hello?" I ask.

She laughs and after washing her hands, puts on gloves. "Because you almost passed out from blood loss, and you need that sealed up right now."

She comes back to me, and I pucker my lips. She sighs but dips down, placing a light kiss on my lips.

"I need more of that," I whisper.

"You'll get your reward after I stitch you up." She takes the remote for the bed. "I'm going to sit you up. Are you feeling okay?" She hesitates before pressing the button.

"I'm not sure why we're not using this bed properly. Come on, baby, straddle me." I tug at the waistline of her scrubs.

"Because you're bleeding." She raises the bed at my back and lowers the portion on the lower half of my legs. I widen them so she can step between them, and she wheels the table over and inspects the cut on my forehead. "There's a chance it will scar."

"Only makes me sexier." I shrug, and she giggles. My hands fall to her hips. "Shut the door. Let's play a little nurse and patient."

She rolls her eyes. "That's for the movies."

"It doesn't have to be. It can be real life too." I raise my hands up her ribs until I cup her tits. "I know how much you love it when I play with these."

She squirms and sprays something on my wound.

"Damn it!" I shout.

"Sorry, I would've warned you, but you were distracted." She gives me a cheeky grin.

I reach around her, smacking her ass then gripping it. "You're playing dirty, but I like it."

"Uh-huh." She focuses on the cut, and she brings out the needle for numbing my forehead before she gives me stitches. This isn't my first injury, and it won't be my last. "Sit tight."

I wince at the discomfort of a needle being poked around an open wound.

"There you go, tough guy," she says, smiling.

"What's my reward if I sit here like a good boy?" I'm hoping she'll take me home and we really can role-play.

"That you won't need a blood transfusion." She positions the needle in front of my face. "Now sit still and let me get this done."

I stay as motionless as possible, but she's distracting me with the way the tip of her tongue sticks out while she concentrates on stitching me up. Her eyes are fixed on the wound, but mine are both on her.

"I was so scared when I saw the bloody T-shirt," she whispers. "I thought you were badly hurt."

"I'm indestructible," I say softly and squeeze her hip.

She leans back a bit and meets my gaze. We both know that's bullshit. Especially with the line of work I'm in.

I ask her what I've wondered lately. "Does it scare you? My work. If..."

She starts working again, but I feel her tense. "Truth?"

"Always."

"It does, but that doesn't change anything. Yes, your job is more dangerous than most, but no one is immune from death."

I steady my hands on her hips. "So it doesn't make you not want to be with me?"

She shakes her head. "No. It is what it is."

"But what if..."

She ties off the thread and grabs the scissors, then drops everything in the bin. "Fisher, I'm finally getting over my obsession over the way we ended up together... the missing fairy tale part of our courtship. So I'm kind of done with what-ifs." She takes off her gloves and places her hands on my face. "I want to be with you. Do you want to be with me?"

I nod.

"Then that's all that matters. I'm done thinking things have to be a certain way or they don't matter. Of course I'd rather have the father of my babies not be in danger every time he goes to work, but I don't want anyone else to be the father of my babies. They'll be lucky to have you."

I slide my hand to the back of her head, pulling her toward me. "You better lock that door."

"We can't."

"Then you shouldn't have said what you just did." I smash my lips to hers with the hopes her libido will shoot off the charts and she'll shut the door.

Pulling away from me, she goes to the door, shuts, and locks it. "You're a bad influence."

"And I bet you're already wet." I take off my belt and drop it on the bed.

She walks over, and I grab the string at the waistband of her scrub pants, pulling it loose. They fall to the floor, and I slide my hand into her panties. Just as I expected, she's soaking wet. We don't have a ton of time.

Our mouths collide and I finger her until a moan slips out. As I'm about to turn her around and fuck her from behind, she falls to her knees and undoes the button of my pants and pulls down my zipper.

My cock flies out, more than ready for her. She stares at

me with hooded eyes, and I cradle her head in my palm. "I'm not sure we have time."

The minute her warm mouth swallows me down, I forget why I was fighting this. She works my dick like she did the other day while I was playing video games—her head bobbing, her hand cradling my balls. The slurping sound alone makes me harder. If we had time, I'd let her carry on, but we don't, so I pull her up. Besides, I don't want the pregnant mother of my babies on her knees on the cold, hard hospital floor.

"Tonight you can finish me if you want." I push her panties to the floor.

She braces herself on the bed, sticking her ass out in front of me. I grip the base of my dick and glide it up her wet core before pushing into her. Her pussy cradles my dick in its warm embrace, and it feels like heaven.

Reaching around, I use my hands to anchor her tits and I fuck her with fervor. Each of us tries to keep the sounds low, but she arches her back and meets me thrust for thrust. As hard as I try, I can't hold off. I need her to come, so I slide a hand between her legs to play with her clit.

She arches farther, telling me I hit the right spot, and soon she falls apart in front of me, but keeps herself stable enough for me to pump in a couple more times before I empty inside her.

I kiss the middle of her back while I gasp for air before withdrawing from her.

"We're going to come to the part where we have enough of each other, right?" she asks, taking a towel from the cabinet and cleaning herself.

I walk over and grab my own towel to clean off, then I take the one from her hand and dip it under warm water before guiding it along her center. "I'm not sure."

"Those six weeks are gonna suck."

"Six weeks?" My forehead wrinkles, not understanding what she's talking about.

Allie shrugs. "Maybe more, depending."

"What are you talking about?" I dispose of the towels in the metal receptacle and buckle my pants.

She's putting herself together while laughing. "After I deliver, there's a period of time when we can't have sex. If I have them vaginally, things need to heal down there. For a C-section, there are muscles that have been cut open and need time to heal."

"Really? How do those people have those kids so close in age then?"

"They get pregnant right after, or they don't listen to the advice. A woman has to have time to heal everywhere."

I nod. "Well, we can do other things, right?" I take her in my arms and kiss her neck.

She rolls her eyes. "Sure, after feeding twins all day, I'll be keen to suck you off." Her eyebrows raise and I clutch her harder.

"Okay, I get the point."

"I thought you might," she says wryly.

I touch her belly. "You feel okay after that? I didn't bang you into the bed or anything?"

She laughs, mostly because I ask every time we have sex. "I'm good, but I really need to get back to work before I get fired."

I take the opportunity to kiss her one more time.

"Now go home and rest," she says.

"Thanks for stitching me up." I kiss her again.

"You're welcome. Now go before we end up having another quickie." She pushes my chest.

I don't want to let her go, but reluctantly I release her, and she pushes me out of the room.

Erin, her coworker, approaches us. "Oh, I was just gonna check on you."

I'm sure she notices Allie's flushed cheeks, always a dead giveaway.

"Sorry, you know Fisher and his need for privacy."

"Uh-huh," Erin says, eyeing us both.

I arrange to be picked up by the new rookie on the force, then Allie walks me out of the emergency room, and I place my finger under her chin, bending down to kiss her one last time. "I'll pick you up at three."

"No, you won't. I'm fine."

A light snowfall is sprinkling down around us.

"I'll be here at three," I repeat.

Her shoulders sag with a sigh. "Fine."

I wink. "I knew you'd come around eventually."

"I think you're drugging me with orgasms," she whispers.

"I could say the same. Bye, babe." I wave and walk through the parking lot to where the cruiser waits.

I stand outside the passenger door for a moment with my hand on the handle. A pain stabs me in the chest, and I don't have to guess what it's from. It's because the one thing I've been most scared of my whole life has happened. I've fallen in love.

Chapter Twenty-four

Allie

The holidays come and I grow bigger. By Christmas, Stella tells me to stop working or she'll put me on bedrest. Because my job requires me to be on my feet all day, I have to agree with her. It's a hard decision, but one that had to be made.

Today is the day of the baby shower. We opted to make the shower a New Year's Eve late lunch with the hopes that we'll be back at the house by nightfall to ring in the New Year with just the two of us.

I never envisioned having a shower at the Northern Lights Retirement Center, but this entire pregnancy hasn't really gone how I thought it would.

Fisher and I walk into the building hand in hand. For a man who never wanted commitment, he's been talking more about our future than I have. I'm reluctant to believe it's true until after these babies are born. Once they're out of me, he won't have to be so protective, since I'll no longer be carrying his most precious possessions.

We walk in the room they use for recreational activities, and everyone who's already arrived—which is mostly his family—rushes over to hug us.

"You're huge," Cam says, and Fisher shoves him in the

chest. Cam trips over his feet and falls, taking down Chev-elle with him.

"Jesus, Cam!" she screams.

"It's not my fault, it's Fisher's." He holds out a hand to help her up, but she's quick to move without help, brushing off her ass.

The room is decorated in pink and blue. There are plastic rattles, baby bottles, and teddy bears, along with confetti on every table. The cake is a four-tier monstrosity that is way too big for a baby shower.

"Dori organized the cake," Ethel whispers as she comes to stand beside me.

"Thank you."

Dori smiles. "Greta owed me, and with the whole apart-ment thing…"

I'm not sure she owes me because of the apartment thing. Things between Fisher and me might've never crossed that line had I not moved in with him.

"We could've had a tier of muffins," Nikki says, coming over and giving me a hug.

Noah is cradled in Logan's arms behind her, looking like an angel. Nikki looks as fabulous as she has every other time I've seen her. I hope my body recovers as well as hers.

"The cake is nice," I fib.

Emilia and Alex, Lucy and Adam's foster kid, run around the room, chasing one another, but Maven is clinging to Kingston's leg.

Fisher ends up going one way and I go the other, saying hello to some of my coworkers. Stella is with them, wearing a pale-yellow blouse that looks amazing against her deep-brown skin.

"You look flushed. You okay?" Stella asks, placing her hand on my forehead as if I'm a child.

"I'm perfect."

"Too much sex," Kingston whispers. "Remember what you were like, Stels?"

She elbows him in the ribs and Maisey whines for a second before calming down.

"Your appointment is tomorrow, right?" she asks.

I don't like the look of concern on her face. I take her hand and squeeze. "I'm fine."

She smiles, but it's a tight one. "Enjoy your day."

"And night," Kingston says, waggling his eyebrows. "If you want to practice…" He tries to pry Maven's arms from around his leg.

"Oh, we'll have plenty of hands-on experience in a few weeks." I chuckle.

I head over to Fisher's sister Mandi, who looks like she could use saving. She's been talking to Midge about her grandson the last little while and Mandi just nods and keeps eyeing me. Shortly after I join the two, Fisher comes over and holds out a plate to me.

"Isn't that sweet?" Midge says. "You're a little soft around those edges, huh?"

Fisher's eyes narrow for a moment. Little does she know how soft and cuddly he is underneath his hard exterior.

"My grandson is like you." She nods to Fisher.

"How's that?" Mandi asks.

"Afraid of the whole marriage thing. In this day and age, you can just get a divorce." She leans in close. "I get that the older generation doesn't believe in divorce, but life's too short to be with someone who doesn't do it for you."

Fisher puts his arm around me and pulls me closer. "I wasn't afraid of the marriage thing."

I shake my head. He doesn't have to pander to Midge by lying.

"So you want to set me up with your grandson who's afraid of marriage?" Mandi asks, sounding confused.

Fisher laughs. I elbow him in the stomach, much like Stella did to Kingston earlier.

"You'd be good for him. Look." Midge puts her arm out toward us. "Allie convinced Fisher she was worth it."

Worth it?

"I wouldn't exactly—" Fisher says, and I elbow him again.

"Thank you for thinking of me, but I'm good on my own. I need to go check on one of the games." With her back to Midge, Mandi rolls her eyes at us and walks away.

"She took it as a bad thing, but I think you're brilliant." Again, Midge leans in as if it's a secret.

I wait half a beat, not sure I want to know why she thinks this, but curiosity gets the better of me. "Why am I brilliant?"

"You got yourself pregnant. Women used to do that back in my day so their parents would force them to marry, you know?"

I inhale deeply and glance at Fisher. He sees that I'm going to lose it.

"We were both responsible for the pregnancy," he says in a firm voice.

Midge gives him an incredulous expression. I step forward, feeling as though I'm going to go to blows with her, and Fisher's hands are on my shoulders.

Midge laughs a second later. "I'm kidding." She laughs even harder. "I just wanted to see what he said." She pokes Fisher in the stomach. "You give me hope that I'll have great-grandchildren one day. God knows Dori and Ethel have me beat. I have to hope for sextuplets from one of my grandkids at this point."

She walks away and Fisher takes me in his arms, walking us into a corner away from everyone.

"She's delusional," he whispers. "If anything, I trapped you." He kisses my lips. "You holding up?"

I nod. I'm good.

Nikki comes over. "Lovebirds, let's go. Fisher, you need to change a diaper faster than Cade and Jed."

"Is this thing over yet?" he groans.

I knew a baby shower wouldn't be his thing, but competition is. I told Nikki not to put him up against Kingston or Logan.

"Okay, everyone. Our first game is who can put a diaper on the fastest." Nikki motions for the three men to take their places on the other side of a table that's been set up with three dolls and diapers.

"I'm the only father," Jed says with a grin.

"Too bad you never changed a diaper," Cade says.

"You got this, baby!" Molly screams from the back of the room.

"Quiet back there," Nikki says in a way that makes it clear she's just kidding around.

I sit in a chair because I'm feeling a little lightheaded. Nikki counts them down and they all start. Fisher hasn't practiced at all. Neither have I. We both think hands-on experience is best.

Cade wins by almost a full minute. Fisher comes in second, and Jed ends up with both of the doll's legs through one hole of the diaper.

"Good luck, Molly," someone in attendance shouts.

Although she isn't expecting—to my knowledge—I wonder about Presley. She's got a water in hand, and the way she runs up to Cade and wraps her arms around him almost feels too emotional for just a baby shower game.

Fisher shakes his head and walks away as if he doesn't care, but I know he's a little sour from losing.

"Hey, you." Stella takes the chair next to me. I see her brain working as she does a quick head-to-toe scan of me. "You sure you're okay?"

"I'm fine. Just tired of carrying all this around." I cradle my stomach with both hands.

"Headache?"

"This morning, but I took some Tylenol, so I'm good. Let's remember, I am a nurse." I rotate my head. I'm just so tired, which is how I am every day now. Add on that I'm uncomfortable because my hands and feet are swollen from the extra weight I'm carrying.

"I think we should plan the C-section," Stella says. "When you come in tomorrow, let's pick a day."

"Can you please be here as my best friend and not my doctor?" I whine.

She shakes her head. "No, I cannot. You could be putting yourself and the babies at risk by waiting for this vaginal birth and I know you don't want that. Let's induce you at the very least."

I blow out a breath. "I have an appointment with my doctor, who I will speak about this with, tomorrow." I put my hands on the table and move to stand, but I fall back down into the chair.

"What just happened?" Stella's hands are out and ready to catch me like she did Fisher when he almost passed out in her office.

"I'm just a little nauseous. I haven't eaten enough today."

"Fisher," she calls, and it's as if the entire room stops.

"What are you doing?" I whisper-shout.

"Taking you to the hospital."

I laugh but stop when I see she's serious. "You are not. I'm fine."

"This is an old folks' home, someone has to have a blood pressure machine here. I'll be back." She races across the room.

"What, are we gonna play a game called guess the preggo's blood pressure?" I say but she's already asking Dori.

"What's going on?" Fisher crouches in front of me and puts his hands on my legs. "You okay?"

"Stella seems to think I'm not, but I swear I don't feel all that bad. She's concerned about my flush."

"You mean your blush." He winks.

"Exactly. Tell her it's because you wouldn't stop poking me in the ass this morning." I run my palms over his face, loving the scrape of his facial hair. Sometimes I still can't believe how far we've come in the past few months.

"I'd rather not talk about our sex life." He waggles his eyebrows. "She's a doctor and if she thinks—"

"She's blending the lines of me being her best friend and patient. She's seeing something that isn't there. Believe me, if I felt that off, I'd know. Now, when are we cutting that cake?"

"Nikki said presents first."

Stella returns, sitting down next to me and short of breath.

"Did you run back to your house to get it?" I ask, but she's busy putting the cuff on my arm. "It's going to be high because you're freaking me out."

"I had to race around to find this. Just humor me," she says.

Kingston comes over, minus the Maven attachment on his leg. I look across the room and see her playing hide-and-seek with Emilia and Alex.

"She won't stop until you let her check you over," Kingston says.

I slump back in the chair, annoyed. "You're ruining my shower."

Stella shushes me. She pumps up the cuff and waits for the reading, tapping her foot.

"What?" I lean over to look, but she moves the screen away.

"It's fine. I just want to do it one more time." She inflates it again.

"You just can never be wrong," I say, rolling my eyes and looking at Kingston. "She always has to be right."

"Tell me about it," Kingston says with good humor.

Once it deflates again, she takes off the cuff and pushes the blood pressure machine away. She nods to Fisher as though they're both in on some secret mission, and he stands before placing his arms underneath me and picking me up.

My stomach lurches and a wave of nausea hits me. "What's going on?"

"We're going to the hospital," she says.

I look around and everyone in the room is staring at us. "Seriously? Was it that bad?"

"Not bad enough that I'm calling an ambulance, but it's high, sweetie." Stella runs her hand down my arm.

Fisher's face drains of color and he looks as if he's about to throw up. I don't think he understands what this means, but I do.

LeeAnn comes into the room with a wheelchair and Fisher sets me in it. Everyone has to push tables and chairs around for her to get through. Another thing that did not go as I planned. Can my fairy godmother find her way to me please?

"Fisher," I say and his hand falls into mine, squeezing it, but he avoids looking at me.

I'm wheeled out and put in the back of Fisher's truck, with Stella climbing in right next to me.

"We're going to Anchorage, Fisher," Stella says.

I stare at her because there's only one reason I need to go to the bigger hospital and that's because something is severely wrong.

Fisher

I knew Stella Bailey was a pretty big deal, but seeing her in action really brings that idea home. She did her residency in New York City and she has a waiting list to see her, but the way she handles Allie and getting her into a room is impressive. She doesn't ask for permission but dictates to the nurse what needs to be done.

"I want two monitors, one on each baby. Hook her up to the blood pressure machine," she tells the nurse, who's scrambling to do everything fast enough. Stella takes Allie's hand. "I'm just going to talk to the doctor in charge, explain everything, but you've probably realized…"

Allie nods and her eyes tear up. "Are they big enough?"

Seeing her like this makes it feel as if there's a knife lodged in my chest and every time her lip tremors, someone twists it.

"They're going to be fine. But we're going to try to keep you under observation. See if we can keep you stable enough to get one steroid shot in you."

It's all over my head, and when Stella walks out of the room, she nods for me to follow, but I stop at Allie's bedside first.

"I'll be right back. Hang tight." I kiss her forehead and she grips my hand so hard you'd think she was an arm wrestler in her spare time. "Are you gonna be okay if I go talk to Stella for a minute?"

"They're coming tonight. I know it." She looks at the screen. "It's my blood pressure. This isn't good." Her head shakes back and forth.

"Just... hang on. I'll be right back." After another fleeting kiss, I rush into the hall to find Stella with another doctor.

She waves me over. "This is Dr. Zimmerman."

I shake hands with him and turn my attention back to Stella.

"Her blood pressure is high, and we cannot let it get much higher, otherwise she'll have to deliver. I'm going to do an ultrasound, and hopefully get her resting comfortably so we can get a steroid shot in her. The problem is that it won't do any good if we have to immediately deliver the babies. We need to keep her calm." Stella looks at me as if I'm the problem.

Dr. Zimmerman says he'll call up for an operating room. Just like that, it becomes clear how serious this is.

Dread is like a pulsing weight pushing down on my shoulders so I can't move.

Stella puts her hand on my arm. "I don't have to tell you that Allie has a very specific way she wants this to play out, but whether it's today or two days from now, she's not getting what she wants. She will not have a vaginal birth with her blood pressure. I cannot have her pushing one baby out, let alone two. So be prepared for her disappointment."

I nod, but I've got nothing. My mind is like a blank page. I have no idea what to do to help. I look between both doctors. "Are the babies in danger?"

Dr. Zimmerman's silence says it all.

"All three of them could be in danger," Stella says.

"That's why I rushed her here. I saw it on her face when she walked into the shower. I think it was just a gut feeling since I know her so well. But she's so damn stubborn about her birth plan. I don't mean that in a bad way, every mother should have a birth plan they're comfortable with, but we have to pivot now, you know?"

At this point, I don't care how these babies are brought into this world, as long as Allie and our children are okay. "Do what you have to."

She nods. "Now go in there and tell her what a great job she's doing. Keep her calm. I'll be right there." She pushes me down the hall.

It takes me a second before I find my footing. The floor feels like quicksand beneath my feet.

In the room, the nurse has turned down the lights. Allie is openly weeping. Oh fuck, I need Stella. I'm not capable of handling this.

"Allie," I say and go to her side, sitting on the edge of the bed and holding her hand. So many wires are connected to her that I can't help but think I'm in the way. The blood pressure cuff inflates again, and I close my eyes, hoping that it's gone down.

When the number comes up, she groans.

"Everything is going to be fine. We have Stella and she's a huge deal, right?" It's the best I've got. I know nothing I say is going to make her feel better about the situation.

Allie looks blankly at me, tears cascading down her cheeks every time she blinks. My chest constricts painfully. There's really nothing I can do to fix this, so I just babble on.

"I mean, I always heard she was the best you can have around here. We have to trust her."

Allie puts her other hand on mine and looks out the

door. She says my name so seriously, my heart lurches and I swallow the dryness in my throat.

"I need you to listen to me," she says.

"What?"

She's stopped crying now and looks straight into my eyes. "If there's a choice to be made… you know, between me and the babies—"

"Stop it, Allie. You're all coming out of this."

She grips my hand harder. "I've seen this before, Fisher. It doesn't always come out the way you want. If there's a choice to be made—pick the babies."

Bile races up my throat just thinking about that possibility, and I have to swallow it back.

"No," I say, shaking my head.

"Please. I want you to pick the babies."

"Stop it. Everything is going to be fine." There's a bite to my tone and I shake my head as if I can scramble all the horrible thoughts inside and throw what she's asking in the garbage.

"You have to listen to me—"

The cuff blows up again and she leans back, inhaling deeply. An alarm goes off on the machine and Stella races into the room, wearing scrubs. She looks at the piece of paper printing out of some machine. Then she looks at the other one. It must be the twins.

She leaves, and a second later, the nurse and Dr. Zimmerman come in with an orderly. They take the cuff off Allie, but everything is rushed as they wrap up wires and talk in medical jargon I don't understand. My hand gets torn out of Allie's to allow them to work.

I step back and watch as a sickening feeling spreads throughout my body.

"Remember what I said," Allie says, appearing strangely calm now. "Please, Fisher."

They wheel her out on the bed, and I follow them through two sets of doors as they scan badges to gain access. I can't believe this. I thought we still had time to prepare for them to arrive.

At the third set of doors, Stella allows the other doctors to wheel in the bed and she puts her hand on my chest.

"No, I'm going," I say frantically.

She shakes her head. "I'm sorry, but you can't. This is emergency surgery. We'll update you as soon as things are stable."

She steps away and I close my eyes. They're burning with tears welling in them. Just before she can get away, I grab her hand to stop her.

"Save her," I say.

She tilts her head as though she wants to make sure she heard me right.

"Save Allie, Stella. If you have to choose." I shut my eyes. "Save her."

It's an impossible choice and one I can't bear to make, but I cannot do this without her. Be a father, exist in this world... it only matters if Allie's here. Even if it means we're left devastated and grieving.

Stella takes my hands. "Fisher, all three of them are going to be fine. I'm going to make sure of it." She steps back and rushes through the doors.

I place my hands on the door and my head falls against it. My entire life is in there. My entire fucking life.

A NURSE CAME and got me, taking me to a private waiting room. I'll have to apologize to her later for my shitty attitude and the things I said. Now, I'm in a room by myself, secluded from all the happy families waiting on news from their loved ones in labor and delivery. I'm in the limbo room. The one they send you to when they aren't sure whether they're going to launch you up to cloud nine or send you down to hell.

"Fish." My dad walks in and sits next to me. "What's happening?"

I bury my head in my hands. "She's in surgery. They wouldn't let me in."

"Yeah, we heard that much. Marla's got everyone down in the emergency room waiting room, but a nurse said one of us could come up."

"God, Dad, what is taking so long?" I sit back and rest my head on the back of the chair, gripping the armrests so hard my knuckles ache. "I should've just listened to myself."

"What are you talking about?" my dad asks.

I stand, unable to sit anymore. "Because I fucking fell in love with her and now she's fighting for her life and so are our babies." I point toward the hallway. "I shouldn't be here. I should've denied it all and maybe this wouldn't have happened. Maybe I wouldn't be hurting this bad."

My dad sighs. "Fish, you don't get to choose those things."

"Yes, I do! I chose not to engage in anything serious because of how much it hurt when Mom died. I never wanted to know that pain again. But something told me Allie was different from the get-go. That's why I never returned her phone call... because I knew. I knew she was special and had the ability to turn my life upside down. Now she might never even know that." I look at him while I pace, hands in my hair, pulling the strands tightly. "God, I'm a fucking mess. This is what I was afraid of and now—"

"And now the woman you love is in jeopardy and you're out here wishing you could go back in time so you don't have to feel this pain. It's not a solution." He raises his voice. "I know where you're coming from, believe me. I've been there. I could barely function after your mom passed away. For years I told myself I'd never remarry. Never put my heart out there again. But then Marla came into my life. Sometimes you don't get to choose who you fall for, they choose you. Or the universe or whatever you want to believe in. You gotta take the good with the bad when you fall in love, Fisher. You get the highs and the lows."

I sit down and blow out a breath.

"You cannot keep running away from your feelings, son. Your mother would be crushed if she knew that's how you were living because it's not living at all. And if you spend your life in love with Allie and your kids, constantly in fear that you're going to lose them... that's not living either."

"But it fucking hurts," I say, rubbing my chest.

"You might not believe me, but the hurt is a good thing. Caring is good. What is life if you don't enjoy it to the fullest? And that means loving someone with every ounce of you. Believe me, when you hold your children for the first time, you'll be amazed at how much love a human being can possess for another."

I stare out the window. Snow is coming down hard. The glass reflects the television, which is on mute, but it's broadcasting New Year's festivities.

"I've let you live with your stupid beliefs long enough, but now you have a woman you love and two kids who are about to come into this world. This is not the time to doubt that everything you feel is real."

"I'm not doubting."

"Something inside of you said to move her into your house, to start a relationship with her. Listen to that now when things are hard. You love her and you love them. That won't change whether all three of them come out of this, one of them does, or none of them. No matter what happens, you'll get through it. The same as you did when your mom passed."

My gut lurches when he says the word none. I never even thought about that, but he's right. I'll be crushed any way this turns out, unless Stella comes out and tells me they're all good.

"I have no idea how you did it," I say to my dad.

"I didn't watch my mom die when I was ten years old. I have no idea how you and your brothers and sister did it, but you did. Ironically, it's the love I shared with your mother that spurred me to try again with Marla. I wanted that feeling in my life again. I love them in very different ways because I was in different stages of my life when I married each of them. They're both in my heart though. But, Fish, being scared of feeling is no way to live. I think you already know that because the chip on your shoulder has disappeared over the past few months."

"I feel like there's an insult somewhere in there," I say, and he gives a low chuckle.

I nod though, because I understand and he's right. It's way too late; I already love her and those babies with every-thing inside me.

The door opens and Stella walks in in a pair of scrubs, a wrap around her head, and a mask pulled down under her chin.

I stand and my dad grips my hand. We both inhale deeply, waiting for the news that will change my life—one way or the other.

Chapter Twenty-six

Allie

My eyes flutter open in a dark room, and it takes me a minute to remember where I am.

"Hey." Fisher's face comes into view. His hand falls to mine and he lowers himself to kiss me on the lips.

I try to sit up, but debilitating pain in my stomach stops me. My hands move to my stomach, no longer feeling the large lump I'd grown used to.

"What happened? Where are they?" I whip my head in both directions and tears gather when I don't see any bassinets in the room.

Fisher squeezes my hand. "It's okay, it's okay. They're good. They're in neonatal intensive care. So far they're doing great."

My shoulders relax and relief washes over me. "How much do they weigh? Are they breathing on their own?"

He sits on the edge of the bed. "They're small. Weighing in at three pounds, twelve ounces and four pounds, six ounces. Both are nineteen inches long. They're breathing on their own, but they told me that could change in the days ahead. They have feeding tubes and I've been Googling way too much shit while you were out. I might qualify as a neonatal doctor now."

I shake my head, but I'm happy to see his arrogance is back. It means the worst didn't happen.

"And you are perfect." He kisses me again. "You had an emergency C-section. Stella says she'll come by with specific directions you have to follow. But the twins are here for the foreseeable future, so you'll have time to heal."

"I want to see them. When can I see them?"

"They really want you to rest tonight." He cringes. "Stella was pretty adamant about it."

"But…" I whine and look at the clock. It's eleven o'clock and I do not want to move into the next year without seeing my babies. "Please? I just need to see them to know they're really okay. Just for a minute."

He blows out a breath and nods before walking out of the room. A minute later, he returns with a wheelchair and a nurse.

"Sweetie, I know you want to see the babies, but we have to take care of you too," the nurse says. I open my mouth, but she stops me. "You're a nurse and you know better than this." Then she smiles. "And if Stella asks, I did not allow this. You two snuck out on your own."

She points at Fisher, and he gives her a thumbs-up. I'm so excited that I try to get out of bed, but once again, the searing pain keeps me in place. Another reason I did not want a C-section.

"Hold on, I'll help you up, but no walking." The nurse walks over to my bedside.

I cross my heart with my finger, and she rolls her eyes.

Twenty minutes later, I'm in the wheelchair and Fisher is acting as if we're really trying to escape.

We reach the floor of the NICU, and he presses the buzzer to gain entry to the area. "My family already came through. My grandma and Dori can manipulate anyone into doing their bidding, I swear. But no one got to hold them yet, they just got to look through the glass."

"They really need names," I say.

"Yeah, they asked me, and I said we didn't know yet. So they're Baby A Greene and Baby B Greene. Thank goodness they aren't identical, cause we might mess it up."

I laugh and clench my stomach when the stabbing pain assaults me. We hadn't discussed what the babies' last names should be, but I want them to share their father's last name. And being a Greene in this town probably isn't a bad thing.

He pushes me down a long hallway and buzzes again to be let in by a nurse. She tells us to wash our hands, and I can't do it fast enough. I'm so eager to see the little beings who have been kicking me for months.

Fisher wheels me over to a little partitioned-off room with two bassinets and two babies who are so small. They have more wires and tubes on them than I'd hoped my babies would have to endure, and it makes me cringe. Now that I'm here, I'm afraid to hold them.

The nurse comes over and smiles at me. "How about some skin to skin?"

"But how do I..."

She waves me off. "I'll get her all ready. You just have to open your gown so I can slide her in."

I inhale deeply and tears spring to my eyes. Fisher grabs my hand and looks at me, tears in his eyes too.

I watch the nurse figuring out which wire goes to what, examining the monitor to check my daughter's oxygen level, heartbeat, and blood pressure. Being a nurse sucks at times because I know exactly what they're worried about.

The nurse takes her from the bassinet and places her on my chest. I hold my daughter and could weep with joy when I feel the warmth of her skin. She has a full head of dark hair and olive skin. She's the perfect mix of the two of us. Fisher and I made into one flawless little package.

I glance up at Fisher and he's got a huge smile. A tear slips down my cheek and he covers my hand that's on her back.

"Laurie," I whisper.

"What?" he whispers.

"Her name... Laurie Greene." After his mother.

"No." He shakes his head.

I glance over to see the nurse preparing our baby boy to be taken out for Fisher to hold. He follows my line of vision, and having no qualms, he strips off his shirt.

"Nice." I chuckle.

"What? She said skin to skin." He grins, then grows serious. "We don't have to name her after my mom."

"I think it fits, but are you okay with it?"

"I'm more than okay with it. Thank you." His voice is filled with reverence.

"Don't thank me."

The nurse places our little boy, who also has dark hair and an olive complexion, on Fisher's chest.

"Where are you going to get their footprints tattooed?" the nurse asks.

Fisher smiles at her. "I still have some blank areas."

He must've told her that when I was still out of it. I realize this is what he was talking about with Liam Kelly, and I smile.

We sit in the quiet, dimly lit NICU and soak in our babies' love and return it tenfold.

"What about this little guy?" Fisher says.

"Axel?" I say the one name I came upon that seems to fit a son of Fisher's. The one we'd both highlighted since neither of us got past the As in the baby name book.

"Laurie and Axel. Axel and Laurie," he says, testing them out. "Perfect."

The nurses bring over some party hats and place them on our heads.

"Happy New Year," they whisper.

"A year ago, would you ever have thought this is where we'd be this New Year's?" I ask. It's been a whirlwind of a year.

"I kind of did. Well, not last New Year's Eve, but that night we slept together."

My eyebrows scrunch as I try to figure out what he's talking about.

"I knew you were different, Allie, and I tried to ignore that pull I had toward you. But I'd never been that jealous, never wanted to make sure everyone knew someone was mine, and it freaked me out. That's why I didn't return your call. And it cost me the first five months of your pregnancy because I was an idiot."

I chuckle and shake my head. "I'm no better. It took me this entire time to realize that what we envision when we're younger isn't always the way it has to happen for it to be right. Sometimes the destination is the more important part, not the journey to get there." More tears slip out. I'd really like my hormones to go back to normal now.

We hold hands as best we can, with each of us having a baby in our arms.

"Happy New Year," he says.

"I can't wait to see what the year brings."

"Me either."

He tries to bend forward to give me a kiss and I try to reach him, but between the C-section and the babies' wires, we're restricted. I blow him a kiss and he does the same to me.

Sometimes things aren't as perfect as you want them to be, but in the end, it doesn't mean they aren't your fairy tale.

Fisher

Almost four months later...

e're at Smokin' Guns tattoo parlor in Lake Starlight, and the babies are being rocked by Allie in the double stroller.

"Fatherhood's pretty fucking fantastic, huh?" Liam, the owner, asks me.

"Yeah, but man, am I tired."

The babies came home a month after they were born, which was good because although Allie practically lived at the NICU in Anchorage, she was able to almost fully heal from the C-section before we had to be all hands on deck. Now we're both getting up every night with the babies. Zoe from The Grind has been giving me free coffee because of the bags under my eyes.

"You have the paperwork?" he asks, referring to the baby's footprints.

I will get the twins' footprints at some point, but there's something else I need to get first.

"Actually, I just want a date and I want it right here." I point at my left pec, over my heart. I have a little bit of space above a rose.

"I thought we were doing footprints?"

I shake my head. "This is more important." I hand him the date and look back at Allie.

Liam's forehead is creased in confusion. "This isn't when they were born?"

"Nope."

I lie down and he doesn't ask any more questions. He shaves part of my chest and prepares my skin for the tattoo.

Allie glances over every once in a while, but for the most part, she's holding a conversation with the female tattoo artist. She's thinking about getting a tattoo herself, which would be her first, but she's not sold yet. I don't want to push her, but I would love to see a piece of art on her that means something about me, whether it's a date, initials, or hell, my name. I know it's kinda caveman of me, but I am who I am.

The needle buzzes on my skin and it only takes twenty minutes. "Easiest tat I've ever given you."

"Truth."

Liam pulls out the mirror and I smile when I see the date on my pec. A day that changed me forever. He puts some ointment on it, but before he bandages it, I call Allie over.

The girl she was talking to agrees to push the stroller back and forth while Allie joins me.

"You're done already?" she asks.

"I am." I point at the date. She reads it, draws back, and reads it again. "Tell me you know what that date is."

She shrugs. "The day you found out I was pregnant?" I stare blankly and she laughs, hitting me in the stomach.

"That day was my rebirth and I have you to thank for that." I wrap my hand around her neck and kiss her until it gets a little heated, and she pushes me away.

"I have some time since I booked you in for longer?" Liam asks with raised eyebrows.

Allie looks at the date and back at me. Then she sits on the bench. "Okay. Same place." Her hands land on the hem of her T-shirt.

"Absolutely not!" I say.

She giggles. "Okay then. Wrist?"

I nod. "Perfect."

"Man, you guys are so cute it's sickening." Liam shakes his head and prepares to do Allie's tattoo.

"I love you," I whisper before kissing her again.

"I love you more."

Then Laurie wails and it's my turn on baby duty. I'd have it no other way. I guess sometimes you get what you want without ever knowing you wanted it in the first place.

ON THE WAY back to Sunrise Bay, we turn on the radio in the car. Nikki's segment is re-airing, so I keep it on since we missed it this morning. Let's face it, getting two babies out of the house is no easy feat.

"My little sister has a boyfriend." Nikki laughs, then sighs. "She's too young, Chip."

"No, she isn't," he says matter-of-factly.

"She is to me, and who on earth falls for their childhood celebrity crush? You can thank me later, Posey. I never thought he'd stick around."

Allie looks at me. "Did you know about this?"

I shake my head and keep listening.

"I didn't think he had it in him to stay here. He makes us all look bad," Chip says. "He's too good-looking."

"He's a heartthrob, Chip. And women all over will be jealous of our little Posey for snagging him."

"I think it was just a date," Chip adds. "You might wanna calm down before you're marrying them off to each other."

She tsks.

I grasp Allie's hand, bringing it up to kiss the inside of her wrist. "Thankfully she's done talking about us."

She shushes me and turns up the volume. I guess it doesn't matter if the babies nap on the way.

"Sparks have been flying between them for months. Believe me, they're going the distance."

"I say we make a wager since you lost the Fisher bet," he says.

I forgot about that bet.

"Come on, they fell in love and had twins."

"You said they'd be married," Chip says, and he's right. She bet him that I'd be married before the year's end. Although my heart is married to Allie, according to the state of Alaska, we are not.

"Fine. Double or nothing."

"Deal."

We park behind the brewery and put Laurie and Axel back in the stroller, which I'm sure they're sick of today. Town is busy and we've been keeping the babies holed up in our house because of the sicknesses going around during the winter. So this feels like their debut to the town they'll grow up in.

My entire family is at Truth or Dare Brewery, but they're crazy if they think I'm stuffing the double stroller in there, so Allie and I wait across the street on the park bench in front of The Grind. Random people stop and peek in, offering their congratulations. One by one, our family members come and join us.

Allie's parents, who I have yet to meet, are supposed to come this summer since they refused to come in the winter.

She has a very different relationship with her family than I do with mine. But hopefully her dad likes me. I've never had to worry about impressing a dad before.

Soon my huge family congregates around us. The babies are out of their strollers and being passed around from person to person. I keep one eye on them, and I can tell Allie finds it funny. She knows how protective I am. She's lucky I haven't taken them all back to the house and locked us inside. The winter was nice, just the four of us as a family.

"Oh, Allie, your apartment," Dori says. "It's all ready."

Allie glances at me.

"Go ahead and put the 'for rent' sign up," I say. "Allie found another place."

Dori smiles. "Just wanted to check."

"We were supposed to talk about it after the babies were born," Allie whispers to me.

"Sorry, you're not going anywhere." I bring her to my side and kiss the top of her head.

"Good."

Loud voices disrupt us, but that's not unusual during tourist season. What is unusual is Posey being the cause of the disturbance. She plucks a sign out of the ground, takes it over her knee, and bends the cardboard.

"What did that sign say?" I ask Allie.

But she doesn't have to answer because two men are putting the same signs up all over the square.

"'Price for Mayor'?" Cade says, his hand on Presley's rounded tummy. I swear his hand hasn't left there since they announced the pregnancy shortly after Allie gave birth.

Marla looks at my dad. Everyone seems confused. Marla's been the acting mayor since Sam Klein left, and we thought she would be running unopposed in this spring's election.

"You son of a bitch!" Posey yells.

Gavin is beside her, holding up his hands in defense. A kid walks by with a milkshake and Posey grabs it from him, then dumps it all over Gavin's head.

"Will Chip take triple or nothing?" Cam asks Nikki.

She narrows her eyes at him.

I never saw Gavin Price being our next mayor, but in this town, anything can happen.

The End

A Greene Family Vacation (Novella)

My Scorned Best Friend

My Fake Fiancé

My Brother's Forbidden Friend

A Greene Family Christmas (Novella)

Lake Starlight

The Problem with Second Chances

The Issue with Bad Boy Roommates

The Trouble with Runaway Brides

The Drawback of Single Dads

Plain Daisy Ranch

One Last Summer

The One I Left Behind

The One I Stood Beside

The One I Didn't See Coming

Modern Love

Charmed by the Bartender

Hooked by the Boxer

Mad about the Banker

Single Dads Club

Real Deal

Dirty Talker

Sexy Beast

Hollywood Hearts

Mister Mom

Animal Attraction

Domestic Bliss

Bedroom Games

Cold as Ice

On Thin Ice

Break the Ice

Chicago Law

Smitten with the Best Man

Tempted by my Ex-Husband

Seduced by my Ex's Divorce Attorney

Blue Collar Brothers

Flirting with Fire

Crushing on the Cop

Engaged to the EMT

White Collar Brothers

Sexy Filthy Boss

Dirty Flirty Enemy

Wild Steamy Hook-up

The Rooftop Crew

My Bestie's Ex

A Royal Mistake

The Rival Roomies

Our Star-Crossed Kiss

The Do-Over

A Co-Workers Crush

Hockey Hotties

Countdown to a Kiss (Free Prequel)

My Lucky #13 (FREE)

The Trouble with #9

Faking it with #41

Tropical Hat Trick (Novella)

Sneaking around with #34

Second Shot with #76

Offside with #55

Kingsmen Football Stars

False Start (Free Prequel)

You Had Your Chance, Lee Burrows

You Can't Kiss the Nanny, Brady Banks

Over My Brother's Dead Body, Chase Andrews

Chicago Grizzlies

On the Defense (Free Prequel)

Something like Hate

Something like Lust

Something like Love

The Nest

Mr. Heartbreaker

Mr. Broody

Mr. S (Title to be revealed)

Mr. C (Title to be revealed)

Holiday Romances

Single and Ready to Jingle

Claus and Effect

Merry Kissmas

COCKAMAMIE UNICORN RAMBLINGS

Fisher might be our most protective hero in all our family series. Well, all our heroes are protective of their heroines, but Fisher had his own reasons to take it as far as he did with Allie. As with the Baileys, the Greene kids all harbor wounds from their childhood. Many of Marla's kids suffered from the divorce of their parents and their father's cheating. While Hank's kids are dealing with the repercussions of their mom dying so young and witnessing her death.

The minute Allie hit the page in Winning my Best Friend's Girl (Baileys #8), we knew she had to have her own story. But at the time we just didn't know where she fit. When we began planning The Greene Family series we decided she'd be Fisher's heroine. Hence the reason you see her in My Beautiful Neighbor when Presley goes to the emergency room.

One thing we loved in this book was that Ethel and Dori were so heavily involved in pushing them together with the issues over at Allie's apartment (you didn't actually think Bert left the house with the toilet overflowing, did you?). And then the U-Haul where they're moving all her stuff over. LOL Can you tell we want to be our very own Dori and Ethel when we grow up? ;)

Not a ton was changed from our original game plan, although we did decide on twins while we were writing the rough draft, which took some tweaking.

We got the idea about the Netflix account recommendations from Piper's husband who watches random shows on other people's Netflix account when they stay at Airbnb's and people don't sign out of their accounts, all in an attempt to sway their algorithm. So let this be a lesson to you all… make sure you always sign yourself out!

As always, we have a lot of people to thank for getting this book into your hands…

Danielle Sanchez and the entire Wildfire Marketing Solutions team.

Cassie from Joy Editing for line edits.

Ellie from My Brother's Editor for line edits.

Rosa from My Brother's Editor for proofreading.

Hang Le for the cover and branding for the entire series.

Wander Aguiar for his awesome job of photographing our Allie and Fisher. Such a hot picture!

Bloggers who consistently carve out time to read, review and/or promote us.

Piper Rayne Unicorns who are our safe place in this crazy world!

Readers who took the time to read our story when there's so many choices out there. We are grateful beyond words for your support!

Posey and Gavin are next. Everyone's crushed on a childhood actor at some point. Rayne's probably aging herself, but Luke Perry (RIP) from Beverly Hills 90210 was hers. She has a signed picture from when she met him and Brian Austin Greene when she was a freshman in high school. Imagine that crush showed up in your town! Just imagine all the delicious sexual tension that's sure to come with these two!!

xo,

Piper & Rayne

ABOUT PIPER & RAYNE

Piper Rayne is a USA Today Bestselling Author duo who write "heartwarming humor with a side of sizzle" about families, whether that be blood or found. They both have e-readers full of one-clickable books, they're married to husbands who drive them to drink, and they're both chauffeurs to their kids. Most of all, they love hot heroes and quirky heroines who make them laugh, and they hope you do, too!

www.ingramcontent.com/pod-product-compliance
Lightning Source LLC
Chambersburg PA
CBHW061245310726
48971CB00007B/2225